MW01519377

Of Shadow and Blood
ALL RIGHTS RESERVED
Of Shadow and Blood Copyright © January, 2023 Tracey
H. Kitts
Cover art by Tracey H. Kitts

With the exception of quotes used in reviews, this book
may not be reproduced or used in whole or in part by
any means existing without written permission from the
author, Tracey H. Kitts.

Warning: The unauthorized reproduction or distribution
of this copyrighted work is illegal. No part of this book
may be scanned, uploaded or distributed via the Internet
or any other means, electronic or print, without the
author's permission. Criminal copyright infringement,
including infringement without monetary gain, is
investigated by the FBI and is punishable by up to 5 years
in federal prison and a fine of $250,000.
(http://www.fbi.gov/ipr/). Please purchase only
authorized electronic or print editions and do not
participate in or encourage the electronic piracy of
copyrighted material. Your support of the author's rights
is appreciated.

This book is a work of fiction and any resemblance to
persons, living or dead, or places, events or locales is
purely coincidental. The characters are productions of the
author's imagination and used fictitiously.

Foreword

Red Riding Hood is one of my favorite fairy tales. If I had to choose, I'm not sure I could decide between this and Beauty and The Beast. Both stories have bled through into my books for years, the majority of which I was not aware of until I finished the books and read back over them. But this book? Oh, this time, it's on purpose. I chose to write this one as T.K. Hardin, because that's the kind of tone I feel suits this particular tale. If this is your first of my books writing as T.K. Hardin, please allow me to explain the difference between this and what I normally write.

Normally, I write paranormal romance under my real name, Tracey H. Kitts. (Technically, this is still my real name just rearranged.) Switching from paranormal romance to erotic horror, as a reader, is not for everyone. So, the name change is to let readers know this is something different. Putting my name on the cover too is to let people know it's still me. This story still has my flavor (so to speak) and personality in it.

But there's violence in all of my regular books, so what's the difference? As Tracey H. Kitts, everything I write takes place in modern times, or in the future. These books do include some elements of horror, but they are strongly romance and less violent on the whole. With T.K. Hardin, everything is historical. I include historically accurate details like language and terminology commonly used, clothing, food, social norms, you get the idea. I also hold nothing back. I recently described the T.K. Hardin books to a friend like this, "It's Victorian Gothic Horror with extra blood, extra sex, you know, all the good shit. We do all the badass stuff you'd expect, but we're wearing corsets."

Although Of Shadow and Blood contains a love story as well, there are also many other elements that might offend readers expecting something a bit milder. As with my other T.K. Hardin books, I didn't want anyone walking into this one without fair warning. Of Shadow and Blood might actually be the most violent book I've ever written.

I'm sure you've heard the story of Red Riding Hood before. You've probably even heard it involving werewolves more than once. BUT, if you haven't read my version, you ain't seen nothing yet.

I am thrilled to present this book to readers and I sincerely hope that everyone enjoys this story as I have. Random side note, I finished writing this book during the full Wolf Moon.

-    Tracey H. Kitts writing as T.K. Hardin

Possible Triggers and tropes: size difference, m/f monster sex, multiple first person POV, intense graphic violence, vulgar language, graphically described monster sex (It's mentioned twice for a reason.), naked werewolves, torture, a twisted sense of humor, light BDSM, and drug use.

Of Shadow and Blood

BY

TRACEY H. KITTS

Writing As

T.K. HARDIN

Chapter One

Belladonna

October, 1801
Viande, France

My name is Belladonna LaCroix and I don't give a fuck that most of the people of Viande avoid me. My grandmother and I hunt werewolves and practice witchcraft. The majority of society does *not* approve of us. Of course, we don't go about proclaiming our magical talents; that would be stupid. Though we are long past The Burning Times, it is not unheard of for a witch to still be put to death. In most cases, however, the women in question usually slept with the wrong woman's husband rather than actually practicing the craft.

Viande is large and prosperous and, according to my grandmother, more willing than most places to overlook our ways. This could be because we serve as healers when necessary, as well as keeping them safe from werewolves. We make a decent living from the poultices and herbs we sell, along with the occasional bounty for the monsters.

I don't care about the frivolous things most women my age are obsessed with, though I don't mind listening when Cherry talks about such things endlessly. Unless they look particularly good, or particularly bad, I rarely notice what anyone is wearing or how they've styled their hair. The majority of the time I wear leathers like a man and I've been told I look damn good in them.

All of my jewelry is silver; it matches my knives, which I wear prominently, strapped to my thighs. My grandmother and I are the reason the villagers get to sleep safely at night and waste time on silly things, like fashion.

This story begins as I was on my way to visit my lifelong friend, Cherry Bonnet, on a crisp and clear October morning. For years now she and I have met once a week (more often when possible) to catch up on gossip, exchange books, talk about men, and drink at least one bottle of wine. Cherry is one of the maids in the castle and is, for some reason that is beyond my understanding, consumed with what everyone is wearing and what that says about them. I've told her repeatedly that most people simply dress according to their station in life and what that calls for. For example, I am a huntress and regardless of what anyone thinks of this, I dress for the job. I couldn't help but think of her when the baker's wife sneered as I passed by.

She looked me up and down rudely and as I walked toward her my leather leggings creaked. I adjusted the silver knives strapped across the front of my corset and smiled at her.

"Good morning, Josette."

Her long brown hair fell over one shoulder in a thick braid and her voluminous skirts flared as she took a step toward me. Josette is only five years older than me, but she's always acted like she was everyone's mother or nurse maid. You know, offering words of supposed wisdom that no one asked for. She's also a prude.

"You can see the imprint of your sex through your leggings," she scolded.

"Ah." I took a deep breath and stretched, adjusting the large basket I was carrying on my arm. "So, in addition to the smell of freshly baked bread, you're also enjoying a nice view of my cunt on this glorious morning."

She choked with indignation as her face turned a shade of red almost bright enough to match my cloak. "I never said I was *enjoying* it."

I thrust my hips toward her and she actually jumped back. "Then stop looking."

Her husband, Rolf, began laughing uproariously at this exchange. Though he immediately tried to silence himself when she turned to glare at him. I say he *tried*, but the poor man continued to chuckle beneath her icy stare as I continued past their shop.

"Tell Islene I said hello," he called after me.

I waved over my shoulder to let him know I'd heard.

Islene is my grandmother and though we dress similarly the majority of the time, no one dares to scold or scoff or even offer a sneer in her presence. Maybe once I've slain a legendary werewolf I will earn the same level of respect.

As I continued my trek, the looks cast my way by the young men of the village let me know that they were enjoying the view Josette found inappropriate.

There are two forests between our cottage and Castle d'Ulfric. The first separates my home from the village by a large enough distance that it takes most people an hour to reach the cottage on foot. That is, when anyone is brave enough to visit us. Though we are not strangers in town by any means, few venture to our home unless it is a necessity. They are also not familiar with the shortest path through the woods that cuts the travel time in half. Most people take the larger and well-worn trail to the left that leads to the woodcutter's house. But to the right is the more direct route that I prefer.

After passing straight through the village there is a stretch of road with several tables and benches and a place for bonfires. This is where our village holds large celebrations and where Cherry normally meets me.

She wasn't there this morning. Given the recent surge in werewolf attacks, this didn't surprise me. I didn't think she'd been eaten, but I did think she was too afraid to make the journey through the woods.

No one is using the word "werewolf" yet, but my grandmother and I knew that's what they were. That is if the descriptions of the bodies could be believed. According to the gazette I'd seen last week from a neighboring village, as many as ten people had already been killed. The current theories are that a madman is roaming from town to town slaughtering people for no apparent reason, or random animal attacks. I suspect it will not be long before we are sought out for our expertise.

On the days when Cherry is running late, I will continue on through the second forest and meet her outside the castle's kitchen. Since this happens at least once a month, I thought nothing of entering the woods, even with the recent attacks, and continued on my way. After all, it was broad daylight and I was well armed with silver, though I did wish I'd brought my crossbow and wolfsbane tipped bolts.

The second forest is sometimes referred to as the dark woods because it is so dense that light barely makes it through the trees overhead. It is vast and sprawls across the countryside for miles to the east and west. But if you continue straight north, the castle isn't very far.

I had only walked a few paces when I caught his scent. Few who are not hunters realize that werewolves have a very distinct smell. You might assume they would smell like an animal, but that is not the case. The more powerful the monster, the better they smell, and the closer to the full moon, the stronger the fragrance. Each wolf smells slightly different, but once you've encountered that scent your body remembers. To those unfamiliar, the aroma I was breathing in might be that of a fine cologne, but I knew better. My nipples hardened against the wool of my tunic and an ache of longing throbbed deep within my sex. Not only was there a werewolf nearby, it was an alpha.

Chapter Two

Belladonna

The last time I encountered a werewolf it was a female and my body still reacted to her scent, though not as strongly, even though I am not attracted to women. My grandmother says this is part of the reason they are so dangerous and also one way the weaker wolves lure their prey closer. Judging by the way my heart fluttered and the wetness of my pussy, this alpha was a male.

Just because I could smell him did not mean the wolf still lingered, but he was here very recently. I paused, put down my basket, and checked my weapons before going farther. I also considered calling my horse, Samson. Even though he was back at the cottage he is bound to me by magic and would hear my call. I reasoned it wouldn't take him long to get here and it would make the trip much faster. The wisest decision would probably be to turn back, but at this point I was genuinely concerned for my friend. Besides that, I *am* a werewolf hunter. Should I really be running from the scent of a werewolf?

"What's in the basket?"

The voice behind me was far too deep to be human. As I turned to face the werewolf I drew a long blade from each of the sheaths on my thighs.

He was huge, easily the largest I'd ever seen. Judging by how high he reached on the tree he was lounging against he was about eight feet tall. I didn't know if I could kill him, but if he made a move toward me, I was going to try.

"Do you know who I am?" I managed to keep my voice steady.

"One of the famous LaCroix huntresses. Your red cloak gave that away. Aren't you going to answer my question?"

The sound of his deep voice seemed to resonate through my body with each word.

"You recognized me? You're either very bold or very stupid."

I'd never seen a werewolf shrug before. The gesture was strange and more human than I'd ever seen a monster appear to be.

"Sometimes, if you get to know me, I can be boldly stupid."

"Are you making jokes?" I asked, taking a step back.

"Are you so opposed to telling me what's in your basket?"

"Wine and books," I said flatly.

He took a deep breath and the sight of him scenting the air gave me a chill.

"I could have sworn I smelled chicken. You see, when I heard the fluttering of your heart, I thought you were a little bird flapping your way through the woods." He ran his long tongue over his lips. "I was hoping for breakfast."

I braced myself as I replied, "If you wanted to eat me, why bother with conversation?"

I didn't realize a werewolf's face could look amused.

"Have you known many werewolves?" he asked.

"A few, none of which I'd consider conversationalists. They were more the bite first talk later type."

His deep laughter rumbled through the woods and I heard smaller animals scurrying for a place to hide.

"Rest assured, little bird, if I wanted to eat you, you would already be devoured."

He shoved off the tree he'd been resting against and as he moved more into the light I gasped. He was even bigger than I'd realized. Standing at his full height, he flexed his arms all the way down to his fingertips before curling inward and then releasing his long claws. He was like a wall of black fur and muscle. He had a neck and head resembling that of a normal wolf, only far too large to be mistaken for one. From his shoulders to his knees he had the body of a powerfully muscled man covered in dark fur so silky it appeared to have been polished. His lower legs and feet brought to mind an enormous wolf standing on its hind legs. To say he was impressive fell short of what it was like to stand in his presence. But there was something else about him that gave me pause.

"Are you wearing trousers?" I asked.

They were darkly colored and in truth only tatters remained clinging to his thighs and groin.

He laughed again but the tone was different, more masculine. "I can tell by your scent that you'd rather I wasn't. But I'm not in the habit of running through the woods, cock out."

"No, you're just in the habit of tracking young cunt through the woods for breakfast."

I don't know what made me say such a thing. I've always had difficulty keeping my mouth shut when I really should know better. But mouthing off at a beast this size? Well, that was a new level of stupidity, even for me.

I'd never seen a grin on the face of a werewolf before, but his was wicked and unmistakable as he took another step toward me. My heart leapt and I switched the grip on the blade in my right hand. This way the sharp side faced outward along my forearm. In a fight this was as much to protect my arms as it was to inflict damage. I shifted my stance slightly as well, anticipating him making a move. But he looked me up and down appraisingly and didn't come any closer.

"Rest assured, little bird, that if I was tracking your juicy cunt through the woods this morning, I would not have asked you to share your chicken," he growled.

"Don't call me little bird."

He opened his arms wide. "What should I call you then, since we aren't fighting and you've made it clear we aren't fucking? That means we're going to continue to talk, correct? Well then, I have to call you something. What about little red bird? Oh, I've got it, little red." He growled softly and said, "Mmmm, I like that."

My body is a traitorous whore. Have I mentioned how the scent of an alpha can be nearly impossible to resist? I'm sure I have, but I don't think my words accurately conveyed the point.

"Oh," he gasped, putting a clawed hand over his heart. "You like that too, don't you, little red?"

"You're just going to stand there, smelling my arousal and taunting me with it? Is this how you treat all the ladies?"

His long-fingered hand remained over his heart and he tapped his chest lightly as he spoke. "Oh, I think we both know that you are no lady, *little red*."

When I gave a derisive laugh in response he added, "I mean that as a sincere compliment. I can think of few things more dull than a proper lady."

"What are you doing out here; because it isn't hunting chickens at the crack of dawn."

"And how do you know when I like to hunt chickens?"

I resisted the urge to laugh at the ridiculousness of his response and instead asked, "Are you the one who's been murdering villagers?"

"Would you believe me if I told you I just killed one of the wolves responsible? That is the reason I am out here so early." He stretched his hands out toward me, but didn't move closer. "It is the blood of one of these werewolves that stains my hands."

"I don't see any blood. Wait, there's more than one?"

He looked down at his hands. "Of course you can't see it, my fur is black and the woods are dark. But surely even your human nose can smell fresh blood?" He stretched one hand closer, but didn't take another step.

"If you think I'm going to put my face near those claws to sniff supposed blood on your hand, you've been hit in the head."

His laughter blended with a growl as he rubbed his palms together, stirring up the scent of whatever was on his hands.

The tang of blood did indeed reach me on the cool morning breeze. "How do I know that isn't the blood of some innocent you tore to shreds or ate in the next village?"

He sniffed his hand and gave me a curious look. "I've been a beast for so long that I'd forgotten you cannot smell the difference." He shrugged again. "In that case, you're going to have to take my word for it." He gestured toward his face. "People see these big teeth and assume the worst."

"What are you in your leisure time, a traveling jester?"

He took a step back and fell into an overly dramatic bow. Seeing a werewolf do this was either going to be the last thing I saw or the most humorous.

"Is the *lady* not entertained?"

I smiled despite my best efforts against it.

"Believe me when I say that if I ever eat someone, they enjoy it. And no one is innocent in the next town over. Have you been to their tavern?"

"What kind of werewolf hunts down others of his kind?"

"The kind who wears trousers asks you to share your chicken instead of murdering you."

I almost lowered my weapons, but instead waivered slightly. "I admit I'm not sure what to do with you."

Not to mention part of me was very afraid that I couldn't take him in a fight.

"We both know what you *want* to do with me, don't we, little red? Such things are not unheard of. I hear that once a human woman has been with a werewolf, she's never the same." As he said this he stroked his cock through his trousers. I couldn't help myself; my gaze followed his hand and saw the thick length of him pressed tightly against the fabric. Even in the dim light of the forest, there was no mistaking the size of his member.

"She isn't the same because she's likely been *broken in half.*"

He laughed again. "I'm telling the truth."

"And where do you hear these things? From the women you've fucked?"

He put a hand over his heart again. "Me? Oh, this is not my usual form for such entertainment. But I've found a few books on the subject."

"You read?"

"I'm not always a beast." He smiled. "Actually, I sometimes prefer to read in this form. My vision is so much better; I don't even need to light a lantern."

"And you've found books about relations with werewolves?"

"Are you impressed?" he asked.

"Maybe just a bit."

"Are you going to share that chicken with me?"

I lowered my weapons. "Maybe."

"So, you admit that you've been hiding chicken from me this entire time?"

I laughed.

"I *knew* I smelled chicken."

Chapter Three

Belladonna

Through this bizarre twist of fate, I ended up sharing breakfast and my wine with a strange werewolf in the dark woods.

I was seated on the thin tablecloth I'd packed with a nearly empty bottle of wine beside me. A half-eaten roasted chicken sat on a plate between myself and the lounging wolfman.

I had taken only a few small bites while he informed me that a *pack* of werewolves was roaming the area.

"Are you certain?"

"So, now you're willing to believe me?" he asked.

He held a chicken leg delicately between his claws and took a small bite. The sight was so outrageous that I nearly laughed again.

"I'm sitting here, despite everything I've ever heard or personally know about werewolves and I'm having breakfast with you. Might as well give some thought to what you say."

"I don't mean you any harm, little red," he said smoothly.

"How large is the pack?"

"I'm not certain. I've tracked the scent of five different werewolves over the last three months. I've only caught one and his was not one of the scents I've come across before last night."

"So, you believe five werewolves, other than you, are out there, doing who-knows-what?"

"At least."

"*This* is ridiculous," I said, gesturing between us. "Lounging around with a werewolf in the woods sounds like the beginning of a bawdy song."

"So you *have* been to that tavern. Well, if you've heard the song I'm thinking of." He put down the bone from the chicken leg and slowly licked his fingertips. "It's all right if you want to fuck me, little red. I won't tell anyone, mostly because I would have to explain that I'm a werewolf. You see, no one knows."

"Are you from around here? Do I know you?" I asked.

"Leave me some mystery, but no, I don't believe you would know me if you saw me in my other skin."

"I'm not going to fuck anyone I just met. And you *are* a monster. I don't care how good you smell."

His smile was sin incarnate. "I was beginning to wonder if I was having the effect on you that I'd first detected. Or if you were simply in a randy mood before we met."

"It's not happening, wolf."

He shrugged and gestured to the open basket.

"Where do you get the books?"

"I borrow them from my friend who works at the castle and she borrows them from Comte d'Ulfric's library."

He raised one bushy brow. "And the Comte doesn't mind?"

I smiled. "He doesn't know. But I take good care of them and return them no worse for wear."

He nodded slowly. "What do you think of his library? Have you learned anything of interest?"

"I've learned the word *pussy* from one of his more lusty volumes."

He had just turned up the bottle of wine and immediately began to choke with laughter.

"I can tell by your response that *you* know what I'm talking about. Any time I've used the word around here I get strange looks. Well, stranger than usual for a woman like me."

"A woman who looks like you and enjoys using every vulgar word she can think of?" He scoffed. "I cannot imagine why anyone would give *you* a strange look."

"Says the talking wolf."

I sipped wine from the large flagon I'd poured for myself. I decided to divide the bottle this way. I was not yet ready to drink from the same bottle as a werewolf.

"I've read several interesting books, but never found anything as salacious as women fornicating with werewolves."

His laughter made me shiver. I was close enough now that I could feel the resonance of his voice deep within my chest. How did I let this happen? When did he get so close to me?

"Anything that good is probably not in the common library. Tell your friend to check the Comte's private collection sometime. If he has such a collection, it's likely in his chambers."

"And you know so much about what is in the Comte d'Ulfric's bedchamber? Do you work with my friend in the castle, wolf?"

"I know what is typical for the private quarters of nobility."

He took a long drink of wine and I couldn't help staring. I'd never seen a werewolf drink wine. Actually, I didn't know they could. He held the bottle close to his mouth, keeping his large fist tight. I suppose that kept the wine from spilling from his wolven lips.

"You do know that well-behaved women don't use words like pussy? They would say quim, if they're feeling daring, but never cunt. Most haven't heard the term pussy. I myself have only heard it abroad or in books."

"I keep hoping that if I say it enough, it will catch on, like a wildfire of profanity."

His laughter startled some birds in the trees overhead. "Today I have met a beautiful and profane werewolf hunter, who didn't kill me."

"Yet." I smiled. "And I've met a charming werewolf who hasn't eaten me."

"Yet," he growled.

My pulse was suddenly racing again and any reaction that had calmed in the rest of my body quickly flared back to life.

"Just let me eat your pussy," he begged.

His voice was rougher with desire and no matter how I tried to control my reaction, it made me want him even more. I took a deep breath as he leaned closer and found myself luxuriating in his scent. I wondered if he even bothered with cologne in his human form.

"You can hold your silver blade to my throat," he offered, sliding closer. "Just please, let me taste you."

He moved closer, towering over me even though he remained seated. Without hesitation my blade was at his throat.

"I don't do things like this," I said breathlessly.

"I should hope not."

My smile was weak, likely because I was both intrigued and terrified by his proposition.

"You really expect me to put myself into such a vulnerable position?"

He reached out with one clawed hand and gently placed it over mine, pressing the blade harder against his throat.

"You can kill me with one stroke at any moment, if I do something that displeases you."

He licked his lips again and I shivered, but not because of the chill in the air.

"I can just imagine the salty tang of your cunt as I split you open with my tongue."

To my horror I sighed and it sounded more like a moan.

"Yes," he purred. "I know you want this."

"What if someone walks this way and sees us? We aren't far off the main road."

He smiled and his fangs flashed in a streak of morning light that made it through the canopy of trees. "That's half the fun."

I hesitated only a moment before I began to unlace my leather leggings.

"That's it," he growled. "Give in to me, little red."

"Take off my right boot," I demanded.

He wrapped one large hand around my ankle and I realized he could snap my foot off like a dead tree branch if he wanted to. I could feel the strength in his grip as he squeezed gently and slid the knee high boot off of my leg. He placed the shoe aside, taking care not to mark the soft leather with his claws.

"Only one?" he asked.

Still holding out my silver dagger in front of me, I raised up enough to slide the leggings down my hips. "There is no way I'm getting naked out here with you."

He laughed as he reached out to help me. "May I?"

"Carefully."

"Don't worry, nothing I plan to do to you will pass on my curse. That calls for a bite or a very deep scratch with werewolf blood on my claws. Licking doesn't count." To emphasize his point he ran his long tongue over the top of my bare foot and I gasped.

"I know that," I said breathlessly. "You *do* recall my profession, *oui*?"

With one leg bare and my leggings down to my thigh on the other, he appraised me with a lascivious grin.

"At least loosen your corset. You're going to need to breathe."

I smiled. "I will not. I'm going to hold this knife to your throat and you're going to eat me, just like you threatened."

"It wasn't a threat. Spread your legs wide for me. Let me get a good look at the pussy you say I can't fuck."

Slowly, I moved my legs farther apart.

"Wider," he growled. "And lift your hips."

"Why?"

"The better to eat you, *mon cher*."

I did as he instructed and when he growled with approval my sex clenched in response. The cool air against my bare skin let me know how wet I already was, if I had any doubts. I don't believe I've ever been so aroused. My cunt literally hurt with desire.

"You'll have no need to attend mass this week. I'm about to make you come so hard you will see the face of God. Every touch will feel like a prayer against your skin."

As he spoke the werewolf lowered himself to the ground between my legs until he was flat on his stomach with his massive head only inches above my exposed sex.

"What makes you think they'd let a witch near the church?"

"Whatever divinity you worship, I can summon them with my tongue."

My laugh came out as more of a startled gasp as he pressed a kiss to my inner thigh.

"If this is as far as I allow you to go, what do you get out of this?"

"I get to recall your pleasure later and touch myself."

I moaned again, only this time, I didn't give a damn.

"Hold it here," he said, moving my knife up farther on his throat. "Any lower and my fur is too thick for the blade to actually touch me."

"But doesn't this hurt you?" I asked.

"Only a little."

He ran his long tongue all the way up my slit and I cried out, arching against him.

"You *have* had this done by a man before?" he asked.

"A man, *oui*. A *wolf*man? This is my very first time," I panted. "Now shut up and get back to it." I pressed the blade harder against his throat as I said this and I swear his amber eyes glowed brighter in the semi-darkness of the woods.

"As you command."

He began to work my clit and my eyelashes fluttered. I moaned again, using the tree behind me to brace my back allowing me to better thrust myself against his face.

He sucked my lips gently as his magnificent tongue split me wide, plunging in and out of my wetness. My eyes rolled and I fought to keep them open. I made myself watch what was being done to me and I kept the knife steady.

"Faster."

"Don't rush me," he growled. He nipped at my flesh and I stiffened. "I will not break the skin. You have my word."

"And I can trust you?" I taunted.

"You're the one holding the knife."

"Faster," I repeated.

He went back to working my clit in faster yet deliberate strokes. I could feel the delicious tension building already. An ache was spreading up my inner thighs up to my lower back. I flexed my arse as I threw my bare leg over his shoulder. I used my other leg against the ground to help me move up and down as I rode his mouth.

No man had ever brought me this much pleasure before. His tongue worked faster than I thought it was possible to move. My empty hand grasped at the forest floor and a moment later I felt his big warm hand over mine, reaching for me. Careful to avoid his claws I twined my fingers through his and gripped tightly.

I screamed as I reached my peak and somewhere along the way I dropped my silver knife. Release flooded my body, shaking me to the core, over and over again. When I at last began to regain my senses I had both hands buried deep in his fur and both legs wrapped around his neck.

"Is someone out there? Are you hurt?" a voice called from the road.

"*Merde!*" I hissed.

The werewolf's amber eyes went wide, but then he looked as if he might start laughing again.

"Can they see us?" he whispered.

I craned my neck for a look, and then quickly ducked down again.

"He can if he looks any closer. *Merde, merde, merde.*"

"You should answer him," he said.

The wolf moved quickly, but he kept low. Maybe the bushes along the road would block him.

"I'm all right," I called back, wiping my soaking pussy on the tablecloth.

"Bella, is that you?"

"You know this man," the wolf said, raising a brow suggestively.

"Shut up, he's a farmer from the outskirts of the village. He knows everyone."

"What did you say?"

Oh, fuck! He was getting down from his cart.

"I said I'm fine!"

I practically jumped back into my leggings; there was no time to lace them. I had just shoved my foot back into my boot when he walked through the bushes.

"There you are. What the devil are you doing in here? And alone?"

"Alphonse," I said, moving my cloak to cover my unlaced leggings. "I told you I was fine."

"What are you doing in the dark woods? Surely you've heard about the recent deaths?" he asked, taking a step closer.

"I'm patrolling the area in search of werewolves."

The fiend had the nerve to laugh from behind the bushes. I coughed to cover up the sound.

Alphonse gasped. "So, you *do* think it's monsters?"

"I do. But there's no need to worry. I haven't found evidence of anything this close to Viande."

He seemed to visibly relax. "Well, it can't be too serious. After all, you stopped for a meal."

I glanced back to where we'd been moments ago and saw deep claw marks in the grass. Before Alphonse could look too closely I walked toward him, ushering him back to his cart.

"Are you on your way to the castle?" he asked. "I could give you a lift. I'm making a delivery to the kitchen."

"That's kind of you, but I should finish up here first. I was just going for my weekly visit with Cherry."

He nodded. "If you're certain then, I'll be on my way."

Chapter Four

Wolf

She returned to find me at the nearby stream. This is where I'd washed the blood from my hands before breakfast and where I was now rinsing her juices from my fur.

She was carrying her basket once again and her clothes had been put to right. But there was no denying the flush still on her cheeks and throat. Anyone who looked closely and knew what they were looking at would know what she'd *really* had for breakfast.

"Your name is Belladonna?" I asked.

"It is. So, you *are* from around here."

"Your family is famous across all of southern France and probably in other parts of Europe as well. And I *did* just hear the farmer use your name."

"My friends call me Bella."

Her smile was radiant. I wanted very much to run my hands through her long braid and set those fiery locks free. I wondered what that mountain of red hair would look like in the morning sun.

"Are we friends now?" I said playfully.

"Well, I don't let my enemies do what you just did."

"You taste like fresh linens sprinkled with salt, with a dash of sweet cream."

I could hear her heart racing once more at the sound of my voice. When an involuntary growl escaped my lips the smell of her arousal hit me again. You'd think she didn't just reach a screaming climax moments ago.

"You don't wear pantalettes?"

"Sometimes I do, sometimes I don't. Today was your lucky day."

I smiled and rather than recoil in terror as most would, she returned my smile.

"So it is," I said.

"I should be on my way, but there is something I want to ask you first and I want a straight answer."

I nodded.

"Why are you hunting and killing the other werewolves?"

"Because it's only a matter of time before someone looks too closely and realizes what I am. As I've said, no one knows my secret, and I don't kill people. The way I see it, me being a werewolf is doing harm to no one. However, if my identity were known, *I* would be the one hunted. Perhaps I would be hunted by you and your grandmother, the famous Islene LaCroix, slayer of The Beast."

"Will I see you again?"

I tried not to let my excitement show when she asked this.

"If you wish, little red." I reached down and tore a strip from my already destroyed trousers.

"What are you doing?"

"Giving you a way to call to me." I used one claw to make a small cut on my palm and grasped the strip of cloth tightly. "A werewolf can smell the scent of blood for miles, and recognizing the scent of one's own blood is quite easy. I will be in the area until the threat is eliminated. Should you wish to see me again for further *conversation*, simply wave this into the breeze. It won't take me long to find you."

I held out the cloth to her and I shivered when her fingertips brushed my hand. The cut I'd made was already healed.

"The exact location of our home is guarded by magic," she said. "After my parents were killed my grandmother worked a spell to protect our home from all who would do us harm. Even if someone drew them a map, if a person was intent on killing us, they'd end up walking in circles."

I moved closer, no longer able to resist the desire to touch her face. When she leaned into my palm I growled softly. Whatever magic she possessed, her spell over me was undeniable.

"As I've said, I mean you no harm. I have no doubt that if you use this at your home I will be able to find you."

"I believe you," she said softly. "I was more concerned about it drawing other werewolves too close."

"It won't, not this far."

"What should I call you, wolf?"

"Yours," I thought. But what I said was, "Wolf works just fine, for now."

And so I watched her leave the woods and return to the road, unable to believe what just happened.

I looked down at my clawed hands. Hours ago they had torn apart one of the monsters that roamed the countryside. And moments ago, they had caressed the face of the most beautiful woman I've ever met. How strange fate can be.

Under the circumstances I wanted to get to know her and had watched her from afar a few times recently on her visits to the castle. I *wanted* to know her, but not yet, not like *this*. She had confirmed the suspicions long held by many, that she is in fact a witch. This didn't bother me in the slightest. Besides, who am I to cast stones? A witch … I wonder if that is what draws me to her like a moth to a flame.

I laughed as I remembered she had also been reading my filthiest books.

Chapter Five

Islene

Preparations for our hunt that night were nearly complete. My blades were sharpened; clothes and silver accessories all lay out across my bed. I was wearing my long black nightgown and considering whether or not I should have my usual wolfsbane tea before the hunt this evening.

As I slid on my boots beneath the gown I decided against taking any tea until after we returned. There's no telling what Bella and I might encounter and I didn't need my strength or speed diminished.

I took a look in the mirror beside my bed and decided to leave my hair down for the time being. Tonight it would be braided as befitted a warrior, but I had other business to take care of first. Royce likes my hair down. I ran a hand through my wild mane and finally gave up on taming my curls.

My hair was still mostly red, even after all these years, with only a few prominent white streaks. Few who knew me would ever guess my true age and I had no desire to tell them. Not that I'm ashamed to be old, for with age comes at least some wisdom. But if they knew how old I really am, then they would begin to wonder why. Why do I look more than thirty years younger than I am?

I touched my side where the bite had long ago faded away. I'd loved Bastian. It seemed fitting somehow that a part of him remained with me. Even if it was the most monstrous part.

Bella had called for Samson not long ago, so it wouldn't take her long to return from the castle after her visit with Cherry. My time was limited. I'd delayed long enough.

I leapt from my window and raced through the woods, welcoming the call of nature around me as only someone like myself can. I heard the sound of an axe striking against wood long before I reached his cottage.

I paused when I caught the scent of his sweat. He smelled of musk, leather, and man, and I breathed him in as I slowed my pace.

The muscles of his back flexed as he continued to split wood, shirtless. Royce Severin is twenty three years younger than me, but in better shape than some men half his age. That's good, because it helps him keep up with me.

His shoulder length gray hair was pulled back and tied with a strip of leather and I smiled as I thought about pulling it free. He was one of the most handsome lovers I'd ever had and as he turned to face me I nearly sighed. His chest and abdomen glistened with sweat, highlighting every curve of his magnificent body.

"Islene," he said, his full lips twisting into a sideways grin.

"Did I startle you?"

"How many years now have you come racing through the woods like a wildwoman, to ride me before your hunts?"

"Is that a complaint?"

He let his axe fall to the ground and spread his arms wide in invitation. "Only if you stop now."

Perhaps it is the beast in me, but even the thought of violence makes me ravenous for the feel of flesh against flesh. Not even Royce knows my secret. He only understands that fighting werewolves leads to fucking for me.

I practically leapt toward him and he laughed, taking a step back.

"Let me wash up a bit," he said.

"Don't you dare."

I ran my hand over his slick chest, reveling in the feel of his chest hair beneath my fingertips. When my hand reached the back of his neck I pulled him down to me, devouring his mouth with my kiss.

"So, you're going out on a hunt tonight?" he asked. I felt him smile against my mouth. "Why does it wind you up so?"

"I never know when it might be my last chance." I began opening his trousers as I spoke, continuing to kiss him between words. "Someday, I might not be the one who walks away from the fight."

"And you want your last time to be with a sweaty woodcutter?" he teased.

"I want my last time to be with *you*. Either way, Royce, you're going to be covered in sweat." Another thought occurred to me then. "Is Perrin home?"

"He's delivering wood to the inn. We have some time."

His son Perrin is a grown man, but that didn't mean I wanted him to find us like this.

"Where were we?"

"You were about to give me the ride of my life," he said, grinning broadly.

Royce has a magnificent body and usually I like to take my time with him. But today I needed this too badly to deny myself the gratification of feeling his cock inside me.

I put my hand against his chest and pushed gently. He followed my lead, all the while smiling down at me, until his back was up against a large tree. I pulled his trousers around his hips, pleased to see he was already hard for me.

With strength a woman my age should not possess I jumped up and grabbed a branch directly over his head. I used this for leverage as I positioned my feet on either side of him against the tree.

"Pull up my gown," I said huskily.

His smile never wavered as he followed my command.

"I don't think you've ever fucked me against a tree before," he purred. "And before you ask, that's not a complaint either."

I lowered myself down as he held his cock steady for me. I took him easily despite his size. Just the thought of him had me already soaking wet.

"I'll do all the work this time," I said as I began to move. "You can make it up to me later."

I rode him hard and fast until my legs shook with the effort. "I'm nearly there," I gasped.

"Here, let me help you."

Royce put his hands on my waist and began to slam into me hard, just the way I like it. I cried out as I came and wrapped my legs around him. He pulled me against him, holding me tightly in his arms as he moved forward slightly. I released the branch and he spun us around quickly, putting *my* back against the tree.

"I can make some of it up to you now," he groaned.

He pumped in and out of me long, slow and leisurely, as if he had all the time in the world to enjoy my body before picking up the pace again.

"I love the feel of your cock," I moaned.

"Is that all you love?"

He slammed into me again and I felt his hot release flooding my sex. I was so aroused by this that I climaxed a second time.

Moments later as we caught our breath he said softly, "Islene, you know that I'm in love with you."

"And you know that I care for you as well," I said.

"I do. But just once, it would be nice to hear you say the words."

I put my hand against his chest and looked into his clear blue eyes as I said, "Royce, the last man I loved, that I confessed my love for ... it did not end well."

"I've learned enough about you over the years to suspect as much," he said softly. "And surely you know that I can relate. After all, we met over the corpse of my late wife, slaughtered by a werewolf."

"Her death is one that has haunted me. I am sorry I could not save her."

"As am I, but you saved *me*, Islene." He took my face in his hands and kissed me tenderly. It was one of the best kisses of my life. "I have mourned her, but that was twenty years ago. I have come to love you very much."

"Don't say things you can't take back, Royce."

When I tried to turn away he held my face still, forcing me to look at him, though his expression remained kind. "That is exactly why I'm saying it. If this is the day you don't return from a hunt, I want you to *know* how I feel."

I took his hands and gently pulled them back from my face. "Royce, can I tell you something?"

"Of course."

"This is something that only Bella knows, and not even she knows the full story. It might change things between us, but I trust you and I want you to know the truth."

"Can we do this over tea? Perhaps with a splash of rum?"

I smiled. "Of course."

"I feel that whatever this confession of yours is, I'm going to need both." He turned toward the cottage, and then turned back to me. "And Islene, nothing will ever change what I feel for you."

As I followed him inside, I hoped that was true.

Chapter Six

Islene

Royce poured the steaming tea into our usual cups before adding a liberal about of rum to each cup.

He sat across from me at the small kitchen table and took a long drink before saying, "I didn't mean to press the issue, about feelings. I'm sorry if I've brought up unpleasant memories for you. It's just that this hunt has me more worried than usual."

"Why is that?"

"It's the savagery of the kills. People are saying that The Beast has returned."

"We both know that is not possible," I said softly. "I put that monster in his grave over thirty years ago."

"I know." He reached for the bottle of rum and poured more into his cup. "I suppose there is something I should tell you as well. You know my friend owns The Salted Pork."

"Yes, the tavern in Pomme de Terre."

"I took him some lumber last month for a room he was going to add. I told you that one of the barmaids was killed. What I didn't tell you was how she was found. Normally, I would have brushed off such stories as hearsay. But my friend saw it with his own eyes. He was the one who found her."

I could tell he was having difficulty with what he wanted to say and likely the memories such a thing brought up for him.

"I have seen more victims of werewolves than I can count. I can say with certainty that seeing them or even hearing about them never gets any easier," I said.

"Her body bore signs of torture beyond the injuries that killed her, and there was no blood near her, except what was on her body."

"So, she was killed somewhere else?"

He nodded. "Whoever murdered her brought her to the outskirts of the town and hung her from the trees in a ghastly display. She was crucified, with her insides pulled out and strung through the trees like decorations. The veins in her arms had been pulled out along with some of the muscles and were wrapped up her arms like ribbons." He paused and for a moment I thought he might be sick. "There were other deep wounds, slashes and bites that *must* be a werewolf judging by their size alone. But such a display also shows the cunning and evil of a man, not simply a beast."

"What you're describing is an alpha who has lost control. Why didn't you tell me how bad it was?"

His blue eyes glistened with emotion as he looked up from his cup, pinning me with his gaze. "Because I was afraid for you to face this monster. Part of me hoped it *was* a lunatic and that someone else would catch or kill them, before you could be hired for the hunt."

He finished the rest of his tea and rum in one gulp, then laughed harshly. "I'm almost afraid to ask what you wanted to talk about now."

I took a deep breath and decided that the best course of action was to simply begin.

"The last man I loved was not who I thought he was. I saw what I needed to see because of the way he made me feel."

Even talking about him now, after all these years, I could still remember the way it felt to simply be near him. The ghost of him still tugged at my heart. However, not wanting to hurt Royce, I kept that to myself.

"I loved my late husband. But before Bastian, it was as though I had never truly known what the word meant. I had never felt such a *powerful* all-consuming love. What I felt for him burned me up from the inside out.

Losing him left a hole in my heart that until I met you, I thought no one could ever fill."

He hesitated a moment before asking, "What happened?"

"My lover's name was Bastian Cheney. But you know him as The Beast of Gévaudan."

His eyes widened in surprise and for several heartbeats he simply stared at me. Finally he asked, "Did you know what he was?"

"I knew Bastian was a werewolf, but I did not know he was the one terrorizing the village of Gévaudan and the surrounding territories." Seeing his horror stricken face made me speak faster. "Please, let me explain. I knew him before he was turned, so that meant he was not the only werewolf in the province of Languedoc. I thought that I could help him. He was a good man and I thought with the right herbs and potions that I could suppress the beast within him … that we could still somehow be together. There are alphas more powerful than most who can live an almost normal life. They are strong enough to truly control their inner beast and not become a monster. I hoped he could become one of them." I took a gulp of rum. "I was wrong."

Royce's hand shook as he reached out to pour us both more liquor. "What made you see him as he truly was?"

"From 1764 to 1767 my family, along with another family of hunters, tracked the monster that had become known as The Beast of Gévaudan. During all of this Bastian not only swore his innocence to me, but he even helped us on some of our hunts and accepted whatever herbs I gave him to try to suppress his bestial nature. What else could I believe? We *did* kill other werewolves during this time. Each time we hoped the nightmare was over, but the murders continued." A choked sob escaped my lips. "He had over six hundred victims, resulting in five hundred confirmed deaths. There are werewolves who still exist as a result of his actions. The guilt I feel for not seeing this sooner … I will take that to my grave."

I gulped down the rum, no longer bothering to pour more tea to dilute it.

"One night he attacked a child that lived nearby."

At this point I was crying so hard that it was difficult to speak, but I *had* to get this out. Once I began talking I found that I *needed* to tell this story, all of it, at last.

"I heard the screams and when I ran out into the snow, there he was." I put a hand over my mouth in an attempt to control my sobs. Then, I wiped my eyes and continued.

"He was half transformed, but I could still see it was clearly Bastian, *my* Bastian, with what remained of this poor child in his hands. I cannot put into words the *horror* of that moment, of how it broke me in every way to see what I should have seen years earlier and saved so many lives. But there it was now, right in front of me and there was no denying the truth."

"What did you do?"

"I screamed. He dropped the child and chased me through the house. We fought as I tried to grab more silver to defend myself. When I reached the back door he leapt at me, now fully transformed. He hit me so hard that we took the door down with us and as we hit the ground, the silver arrow in my hand pierced his heart."

"Dear God." After a pause he said, "I'm sorry."

"There is more. It wasn't until after I had crawled from beneath his body that I realized he had bitten me during the fight." I wanted to see his reaction to this, but couldn't bring myself to look him in the eye until I was finished. "I know that sounds insane, but he was throwing me around so much that I didn't even feel the bite. I immediately cleaned my wounds with a mixture of wolfsbane diffused in holy water. Pouring the concoction on that bite hurt worse than bearing a child. But when that agony had passed, the bite healed at a normal, almost human rate. Almost."

Now I did look at him and was unprepared for what I saw. Not only compassion, but perhaps understanding. He reached over and took my hand.

"I knew you were stronger, faster than you should be. I'd always assumed it was due to your magic." He hesitated before asking, "Are you telling me you are a werewolf?"

"No," I said quickly. "And I have certainly *not* been killing people. I am something in between. What I did that night prevented my transformation, and I continue to drink wolfsbane tea to prevent changing."

"And you've told this to no one but Bella, in all these years?"

"My daughter was already married and lived in another village at the time, so I never confided in her. My cottage was remote. To others my relationship with Bastian was barely a rumor. They only knew that we were acquainted. Bella knows I had a lover who was a werewolf and he bit me. She does *not* know that he was The Beast."

"There will always be rumors about women who work with herbal medicine," he began carefully. "Yet you trusted me to know that you truly are a witch, more than a decade ago. And you kept this to horror to yourself."

My throat was tight with emotion, so I only nodded in response.

"What a burden to carry," he said softly.

"If people knew, I wouldn't be a heroine anymore. They would hate me, blame me for all those deaths. Perhaps they should. Bastian attacked roughly three hundred people a year for three years. That's about twenty five a month. And I knew *nothing*. It didn't occur to me until after his death that I never saw him during the three days considered to be the full moon. Many people think the full moon is only one night, but that isn't true. Only the *height* of the lunar cycle lasts one night. It's like the cycle of life represented in the goddess, the maiden, the mother, and the crone. What most considers the full moon is the phase of the mother." I shook my head. "I didn't mean to ramble on about the damn moon. The point is, I should have *known* something, *seen* something during those three years."

"Did you live with him?" he asked.

"No. We saw each other perhaps once a week. He lived a few hours ride from me."

"Then you certainly could not know everything he did. If my wife had been the one in his place, telling me she was not a monster, I would have believed her. I would have *chosen* to believe her."

"You don't hate me or blame me?"

"I could never hate you."

"The night before I killed him, I told him that I loved him. I'm sure he knew the depth of my feelings, but it was the first time I actually said the words. And the last time I've said them to anyone."

"My poor Islene," he said softly.

Royce took me in his arms and for a long time I simply let him hold me while I cried.

At last I pulled back, relieved to see he looked at me the same way he did before my confession.

"I should go. Bella will be back soon. She doesn't even know we've been hired for the hunt yet."

"Perrin should be back soon as well. It's a shame things didn't work out with him and Bella," he said.

I was so relieved to have a lighter subject to talk about once again.

"I think he's interested in her friend now, Cherry."

"The tart at the castle?" I smacked him playfully and he laughed. "What? She is a tart."

"*You* are a tart, Royce."

"You say that like it's a bad thing."

"I've always loved a good tart."

As I turned to leave he said softly, "Islene?"

"Yes?"

"You can trust me with your secret. And you could have long before today."

"Thank you."

Chapter Seven

Cherry

I came down to the kitchen, lured by the scent of Armand's famous apple pie. Yet here I was with *my* pie the one being eaten.

Armand seemed ravenous upon seeing me walk through the door. He sent the rest of the kitchen staff out and threw up my skirts with barely a word spoken. I moaned as he devoured me. I couldn't see his head beneath my skirts, but by God I could feel him.

He stood up suddenly, gasping as he wiped my juices on the back of his sleeve.

"Let me fuck you," he begged. "I need to be inside you."

He reached beneath me and lifted me farther up onto the worktable.

"There is flour on my arse," I said, laughing.

"It will wash."

There was no time to object, not that I planned to, before he bunched my skirts up higher and thrust his cock deep inside of me. The table rattled with the force of his thrusts as I leaned back against the small window behind us and shoved my hips toward him.

Armand is a fantastically good fuck. Perhaps I should break off my involvement with him, now that I've started courting Perrin. But something about keeping this a secret makes his cock feel even better.

"I think I hear someone outside," I said, breathlessly.

"I don't hear anything." He reached between our bodies and began to work my clit.

"But, Armand, I could have sworn someone called my name."

He took a wad of my skirts and shoved them into my mouth. "The door is locked. Now be quiet and take this cock like a good girl."

I love it when he puts me in my place. The instant he touched my clit again I started to come. I screamed around the cloth in my mouth as I thrust my quim against him, begging him with my body to give me more.

"See, I knew you needed this too," he growled. "Let me give it to you."

Moments later while he was still pumping me, I *knew* I heard someone call my name. Armand cried out with release as I turned just enough to see Bella outside the window, laughing.

When Armand noticed her, he laughed as well.

"Something tells me that of all people, Bella will not be offended by this," he said, pulling away from me.

"Give us a moment," I called through the door.

After tidying ourselves up I turned to Armand and said, "I expect a slice of that pie when I return."

He looked me up and down lasciviously. "I could say the same to you."

"You've already had yours."

When I opened the door Bella was now sitting on top of the table the kitchen staff liked to use on beautiful days to have breakfast.

"There are four perfectly good chairs," I said, smiling.

"The table is more comfortable."

"I thought you weren't coming today."

"Apparently you are though," she teased.

"Slut," I joked.

"Says the woman who is *supposed* to be involved with Perrin these days. At least I know why you didn't meet me at our usual place."

I joined her, sitting on top of the table, and opened the basket beside her. "I didn't meet you because I thought you'd be getting ready for the hunt."

She gave me a confused look.

"You haven't heard? The mayors of Viande, Pomme de Terre, *and* Gévaudan, got together and decided to hire the infamous LaCroix women to hunt down the source of the recent murders."

"The source? You mean werewolves, as I've said for the past few months."

"Either way, the mayor has probably already gone to your house and spoken to Islene. You, my friend, are hunting werewolves tonight."

She stretched and smiled. "Good. I was starting to crave a fight. How do you already know about this and I don't, considering *I'm* the huntress?" As she said this Bella gave my long blond braid a playful tug.

"The same way I know lots of things. I'm nosy and I spy on the rest of the staff."

She laughed as I took the books from the basket. "What did you think of these?"

"Oh, your tea is in the blue pouch, before I forget. As for the books, this one was excellent," she said, pointing to one thick volume. "The other one, the hero was an idiot. Does the Comte have a private collection of books?"

I shrugged. "He probably does, but I've never been in his chambers. Much to my disappointment, he doesn't dally with the staff. Speaking of the Comte — "

"No, let's not. I'm not sure how I feel about that."

I shrugged again. "As you like, but he *is* very handsome. If you wanted to get a look at him, you can always stay with me for a while on a day when you have more time."

"You've made that offer before and I wasn't interested, remember?"

"You need to *get* interested, Bella. I fear you have little choice. May as well enjoy yourself, eh?"

Bella reclined onto her elbows. "He has decent taste in literature, so at least he's intelligent."

"And quite formidable, in a dashing sort of way."

"You think everyone is dashing," she joked.

"Ah, but Maroc d'Ulfric is a different breed entirely. Trust me." I sighed and looked at the bundle of tea on my lap. "If I tried to grow the herbs for this myself, do you think I'd get burned as a witch?"

"Only if men and self-righteous women figured out what it's used for. If it makes you feel better, you're far from the only woman around here who comes to my grandmother for this tea."

"The way I enjoy men, I can't take chances on every encounter bearing fruit," I said.

I put the tea aside and lifted the wine bottle, shaking it gently. "Why is this empty? Did you drink it all on the way?"

Bella laughed. "Ah, I was getting to that part. You will never believe what happened to me when I went into the dark woods today."

"I still can't believe you came all this way, with everything that's been happening around here."

"Samson is waiting for me at the stables, so it won't take me long to get home."

I love her big beautiful horse. He is solid black with a mane that is more lovely than that of any woman's. I've always wondered if he was made of magic. Of course, only a few of us know that the whispers about Bella and Islene are true. They don't merely deal with herbs and medicines; they have *real* power. The Comte is among those who know her secret, even though he and Bella have never met. That's probably why her grandmother chose him, because the d'Ulfric family was once in the same business. That would be werewolf hunting, not witchcraft.

Bella seemed to hesitate before saying, "I've heard of other women who took a werewolf as their lover."

I nearly choked. "Is that what you were thinking about when you drank an entire bottle of wine in the woods this morning?"

"No. That's what I was thinking about on the ride to the castle, after I shared my wine and my pussy with a werewolf in the woods."

For a moment all I could do was look at her with my mouth open in surprise.

"For goodness sake, say something," she said.

"You're going to give me details and I'm going to get us a fresh bottle of wine." After sneaking a bottle from Armand's private cache, I took a large gulp and passed Bella the bottle. "All right, tell me what it was like to fuck a werewolf." Before she could answer I said, "Really, Bella!? When they're out there killing people? This is how you spend your time?"

"First of all, I don't think he had anything to do with that, and second, I didn't fuck him."

While I drank nearly the entire bottle of wine my friend proceeded to tell me about the most scandalous exchange I could imagine. When she had finished talking I continued to drink and stare at her.

"Well, aren't you going to say anything?"

"That's quite a change from the traveling minstrel you were with last month," I said at last.

We both started laughing.

"I can't believe what I just heard," I said. "Are you having a laugh at me or did this *truly* happen?"

"I can scarcely believe it, but I assure you, it happened. I honestly don't believe he is a killer, at least not of humans. He claims to be hunting the werewolves responsible for the recent murders. He said he does so to keep his secret safe. That sounds like as good a reason as any to me. If I were in his position, I'd certainly want to protect my identity."

"There's something I've never asked you in all these years. Where did they *come* from, werewolves I mean? Those who know of their existence try to pretend it isn't real. Unless they've seen a monster first hand, no one believes they exist." I paused for another drink. "Except for those of us whose best friend hunts them," I added with a smile.

"My grandmother says werewolves are the result of a curse from long ago, made of shadow and blood."

She took the bottle from me and in one go finished off its contents.

"Could you truly not resist him?" I asked.

Bella laughed and I couldn't help but admire how lovely she was. I have always thought my friend to be one of the most beautiful women I've ever met. That includes the nobility that has visited the castle since my employment here. There is a grace and dignity about the way she carries herself that would fool anyone into believing she is a high born lady. That is until she speaks to them and starts trying to convince them they should use the word pussy, because she read it in a naughty book. Bella delights in shocking people, especially any she deems to be a prude. I truly love that about her.

She pulled her red cloak close to her face and breathed deeply. "Here," she said, pushing the fabric closer to me. "You can still smell him."

"You want me to sniff a werewolf?"

"Just do it."

I breathed deeply and sighed. "Do werewolves wear cologne? They are partially human, after all, right?"

"I don't think he needs to bother with cologne. Each werewolf has a unique smell. My grandmother has always told me that the stronger the wolf, the better they smell. He must be the most powerful alpha I've ever met, because none of them have *ever* smelled like this before, nor had such a power over me."

I leaned over and sniffed her cloak again and sighed. "It smells similar to a cologne I've noticed when the Comte has passed me in the hallway."

"Do you think the Comte also romps in the woods with werewolves?" She barely said this before bursting into laughter. "I'm joking. It's nice to know the man I am stuck with does at least bathe and smell nice."

I gave her what I hoped was a scolding look. "We should all be so fortunate. He's amazing from what I can tell. I don't know a woman alive who wouldn't tear out your hair to get near him. Besides that, you've had twenty five years to choose your own, and you haven't."

She laughed again. "I'll have to see this for myself soon enough. But in the meantime, what am I to do about Wolf?"

"You believe he might be from around here?" I asked.

"I think that is a good possibility."

"Will you summon him as he said you could?"

"I think I will."

"Will you tell Islene?"

"I tell her most things."

"And what of the Comte?"

"One thing at a time."

"Cock," I said.

She laughed. "What?"

"I think you meant one *cock* at a time."

Chapter Eight

Belladonna

The wind blew my braid loose as Samson galloped headlong past the outskirts of the village, directly to my shortcut through the forest. I leaned down and whispered my thanks in his ear, knowing he understood. I really didn't feel like walking all the way back. And if I was being honest with myself, I was wary of encountering the other werewolves I knew were not far away.

When we reached the cottage I smiled, as I often do at the sight of home. Grandmother has always referred to it as a cottage, though it is large enough to be called a chateau by some. Our home was built by the lords who ruled this land before the d'Ulfric's and is quite large, though not a castle. It is made of wood rather than stone and looks like an enormous cottage that someone continued to add onto for quite a while. This is where the ruling family lived until the castle was built.

Our home rests against the corner of the woods. The large embankment behind protects us from the majority of storms, and the two massive oak trees to the left both grow through and hold up our barn. I was small when I moved here with her, but it feels as if I have always been in this place, on this land.

I walked Samson to the barn and saw that he had food and water.

"I'm sure we'll be going out again soon," I said to him, stroking his dark head. "Maybe you should take a nap."

The first thing I noticed when I walked through the door was her hair. The braids were a magnificent tangle of pale red and white, pulled tight across her temples and hanging in a thick cord that reached past her waist. Her hair alone would have told me we'd been hired to hunt, even if Cherry hadn't said a word.

I grew up knowing Cherry's grandmother and as I looked at mine now, dressed head to toe in tight black leather, the comparison was almost comical. She turned to me and I saw her eyes were lined heavily with kohl as well. She looked dangerous and primal, and as always, beautiful.

"I hear we've been hired," I said. "When do we leave?"

She slid a knife into her belt and nodded. "Within the hour, if you can manage it."

I opened my arms, holding my cloak wide. "Am I missing something besides a few more knives? I can be ready much sooner than that."

She walked toward me and sniffed my shoulder before pulling back with a knowing look. "You reek of werewolf, a strong alpha, unless my senses deceive me."

I felt my face flush with the memory of what happened in the dark woods.

"I was going to tell you about that."

"I'm not judging you, Bella," she said softly, turning back to her weapons on the table. "I'm only saying you should change your clothes. Your scent might cause unnecessary attention from our quarry, giving them the upper hand." She paused, then turned to face me again. "Be careful, *ma chérie*. I speak from the heart, not to chastise your desires."

"Can I talk to you about it while I change?"

"Please do." She walked over to her workspace beside the kitchen and brought back a small bottle of oil. "And use this. It will hide our natural scent as well as any lingering traces of wolf."

"I take it you're already covered in this?"

She smiled. "Of course I am."

While I told my grandmother what happened to me today I changed everything I was wearing. Fresh leggings, tunic, and corset. I even changed my tight camisole. I had several specially made to be tight enough to hold my breasts firmly. This was something my grandmother recommended years ago and had helped greatly with my fighting. My breasts aren't overly large, but no one wants a tit flying free when they're trying to fight monsters.

In order to help hide us against the night, everything we wore on a hunt was black, except for our red cloaks. For humans who saw us, this established us as LaCroix hunters. For werewolves, the cloaks helped to grant us a small amount of magical protection. The dark red wasn't so easily seen at night either.

By the time I was strapping knives to my thighs again I had told her everything. I left out the more explicit details I'd given to Cherry. Islene and I have always been very honest with each other, but she is still my grandmother and there are some things I would not say to her. However, that does not mean she isn't clever enough to figure out all the things I didn't say.

"Be sure to leave the cloth with the blood in your room," she said. "Lock it in the big cedar chest to hide the scent unless you intend to use it."

"I will."

"Any creature intent on harming us wouldn't be able to follow the scent into the woods. But it might lead your wolf here at a time you didn't intend. You *do* mean to call him at some point?"

"Yes."

"Are you certain that's wise?"

"Because he's a werewolf?"

"Because you will likely be the bride of the Comte d'Ulfric within a month's time."

For a moment we simply looked at each other and I saw sadness in her eyes.

"Is that all you have to say about the matter?" I asked softly. "Aren't you going to tell me how foolish I am? That after all you've told me, after the werewolves we've fought together, I should *never* have let my guard down? Should I have killed him on sight? He was enormous, but shouldn't I have at least *tried*? Isn't that what a hunter is supposed to do?"

"Do you trust him?" she asked.

I hesitated.

"What I'm asking is do you believe he is hunting them also and not a part of their pack?"

"I do. Beyond that, I'm not certain."

"I've spent years teaching you to trust your gut, so trust it."

"I am very drawn to him, physically."

She laughed, but not as though she was truly amused. "Believe me, I *do* understand. Come with me."

I followed her down the hallway and into her bedroom. There is a large trunk at the foot of her bed, mostly filled with weaponry and dried herbs, along with our family grimoire.

I watched as she took out a black leather pouch and began to pull out a silver chain. It was thin and reflected the light streaming in through her window like a captured star.

"This is made of the finest silver. It is only because of the incomplete nature of what I am that I can touch any silver at all. But this is so pure, I do feel some small amount of pain when it touches my bare skin." She slid the chain back into the pouch and handed it to me. "This was part of my payment for killing The Beast. Use it wisely."

"I don't understand."

"There is ten feet of chain. Use it to restrain him until you are certain you can trust him."

My eyes widened. "Are you suggesting that I—"

"Fuck him," she said bluntly, and laughed again. "If you think you can control him, or if he can control himself." She reached out and squeezed my shoulder gently. "But be careful and be warned. You know what happened to me."

To emphasize her words her normally warm brown eyes bled to wolf amber. In a blink, they were brown again.

"Shouldn't a woman's grandmother tell her to remain pure until marriage?" I joked.

"You and I both know that time has passed. As for the Comte, if he wants purity, he should not be looking at the LaCroix women at all."

I embraced her suddenly and she held me tightly in return. Even at her age there is nothing soft about her. I could feel the strength in her arms and the hard muscles of her back.

"I love you," I said softly. "Now, where do we ride?"

Chapter Nine

Belladonna

An hour later we had the horses saddled and loaded with supplies for a four day hunt. Samson carried most of the weapons because he was bigger and stronger. My grandmother's gray speckled mare, Cleo, carried the other items we'd need to make camp.

"According to the latest I've heard, two bodies were found on the far outskirts of Pomme de Terre." She pointed to a map spread out on our kitchen table. "That's a two day's ride. But just because the bodies were found there doesn't mean the werewolves haven't moved on."

"They're getting too close to home," I said.

"Far too close. There is only one thing left to do." She passed me a rope of braided sage and a clear crystal on a chain. "This is your gift and my senses are mine. Point us in the right direction and I will track them down."

We had already cast the circle before laying out the map. I repeated an incantation as I lit the sage and began to walk the circle, letting the fragrant smoke fill the air. After completing the circle I placed the sage in a large sea shell and passed the crystal through the smoke.

I focused all of my intention on finding the right trail, on stopping these monsters before saying aloud, "Where are the werewolves we are looking for?"

I let the chain unfold from my palm until the crystal was hanging directly over the middle of the map. It spun in ever widening circles until stopping firmly right beside Pomme de Terre in the middle of a small forest.

"Now we ride," my grandmother said, taking up the map and tucking it into the pouch on her side.

We snuffed out the sage and within minutes we were racing through the woods and toward our first werewolf hunt in almost two years.

"Things were quiet for so long, I'd begun to hope for retirement. He told you there were as many as four?" she asked as Samson fell into step beside Cleo.

"At least. He said he tracked the scent of four different werewolves, besides the one he killed sometime last night."

"If we are unfortunate enough to find them all together, this will be the most either of us has faced at once," she said. "Do you feel you are ready?"

"After all the hours of training, if I'm not I never will be. How many have you fought at once?"

"Two and they nearly killed me. That was about a year before your first hunt."

"In the ten years I've hunted with you, we've only killed seven. And now there are four out here at the same time? That can't be good."

She nodded. "If your wolf can be believed there were five until last night. This means there must be an alpha on the move, and he or she is growing their pack. For what purpose, I can't imagine. It's a shame the Comte gave up hunting after his father was killed. We may need the help."

We entered the village and though we slowed our pace everyone turned to stare. The road through town was the most direct route to the road to Pomme de Terre. We really couldn't avoid this if we wanted to make good time. Still, everyone knew what this meant. Seeing us with our red cloaks, black clothes, and silver weapons on our horses. Not to mention the fearsome cosmetics my grandmother insisted upon.

She caught me looking back at the villagers who stared and said softly, "They're scared.

From what Royce told me today, they should be."

"They could try being grateful, for once. You know, just a, 'Thank you that my fat arse isn't out tracking down monsters. Oh, thank you Bella and Islene for protecting my lazy arse.'"

She snickered. "Don't be cruel, child. They have not lived the lives we have. Most of them truly do not understand. And they *do* thank us."

"How so? I've never heard a thank you."

"They pay us."

The sun was setting as we left the village and turned onto the open road that would eventually lead to Pomme de Terre.

My grandmother kept looking at me and I knew she had something to say. Finally I asked, "What's on your mind?"

"A messenger brought another letter for you this morning, from the Comte. If you'd taken the common road you probably would have ran into each other."

"And?"

"He has requested us to join him at the castle to celebrate your engagement and to set a date for your wedding. I took the liberty of answering on your behalf."

"What did you tell him?"

"I sent a letter back, telling him that we would send word as soon as we returned from this hunt. I imagine he will want to have a feast as soon as possible after that." She was quiet for several moments before saying, "There is a reason this arrangement was made. However, after you meet him, if you truly find him distasteful, I can find a way out of our agreement. You do not have to marry a man you despise. I would never do that to you."

"I know you wouldn't," I said softly. "And I understand why … Maroc and I are all that remains of two once large families of werewolf hunters."

"And his father was my dear friend. I can scarcely believe he's been dead for five years now." She smiled then. "I believe that's the first time I've ever heard you call the young Comte by name."

"Well, I don't know him."

"You have chosen not to know him."

"He stayed busy with his father, traveling and hunting werewolves."

"But he retired five years ago," she said, arching a brow.

"I wanted to see if there was anyone else that interested me before I …"

"Was stuck in an arranged marriage? I understand. What if you become attached to your new *friend*?"

"That's a very good question for which I don't yet have an answer."

She laughed, then took a deep breath. I knew she was beginning to search for a scent.

"Anything?"

"Not yet."

"Did they ever catch the werewolf who killed Maroc's father?"

"Maroc finished off the werewolf trying to save him, but Vallis died of his wounds before he could return home."

"His injuries must have been truly grievous. Otherwise he would have become a werewolf and started to heal, right?"

"Vallis would have taken his own life before allowing himself to turn. I've often wondered if that is what happened and Maroc didn't have the heart to tell anyone the truth. The same thing that is happening now happened five years ago, and ultimately led to the death of my friend."

"What do you mean? I don't remember hearing about so many werewolves this close to home."

"That is because they were much farther north and I didn't tell you the details."

I gave her a questioning look.

"That was the winter when Royce had a bad fever and I stayed with him for a week."

"Yes, I remember."

"Vallis showed me the messages he'd received, asking for help. He had a theory that a powerful alpha was forming a pack. He thought they were traveling, seeking out weaker werewolves to join them."

"That's terrifying."

"He invited us to join them, but I was afraid to leave Royce, or of sending my only living descendant on a hunt without me. If I had gone with them — "

"Then your lover might have died without your help. There is no doubt in my mind that your potions saved his life. You cannot blame yourself for your friend's death."

"But I do," she said softly. "After his father's funeral, Maroc told me they found a den of ten werewolves."

I gasped.

"They had been joined by two other hunters that lived closer to the area. Both were killed."

"And the rest?"

"Nine were killed, including the alpha. One escaped and has never been found."

"You know as we are setting off on a hunt, and it is now fully dark, that has to be the *worst* story you could possibly choose to share."

To my surprise she laughed. "I'm sorry, *ma chérie*. I've never exactly been cheerful company."

This was true. But she had been through a lot, much I was aware of and much that I was not. I couldn't blame her for being somewhat grim.

"We should set up camp for the night," she said.

"Already?"

"We've been riding for hours and my arse is sore. We'll find a place off the road, so any travelers won't bother us."

She stopped for a moment and sniffed the air again.

"Werewolves?" I asked.

"A fire. Someone else is camping not far from here." She sniffed again. "And they're cooking venison."

She turned Cleo off the road and I followed her into the woods. "We won't get close enough to bother them and we'll leave early."

"Should I start setting up the camp or hunt for dinner?" I asked.

"You start the fire. I can see in the dark."

When we came to a stop I took a deep breath and smelled absolutely nothing. Grandmother looked at me and smiled as if reading my thoughts.

"They are not close enough for human senses to detect."

"It's a little scary when you say it like that, even if you are my family," I joked.

Her eyes lit up in the darkness as she replied, "I smell rabbits. Be right back."

Chapter Ten

Belladonna

I woke with a start. I could have sworn I heard a scream. I had almost convinced myself it was a dream when I saw my grandmother on the other side of what was left of the fire.

She looked at me with her eyes glowing bright and pressed a finger to her lips for silence.

A piercing cry shattered the night. It was the most horrific, anguished sound I'd ever heard and my blood ran cold as the scream echoed through the woods.

"Grab your weapons and silence the horses," she whispered. "We travel light and silent. We may still be able to save someone."

I got up as fast as I could and put one hand on Samson's head and the other on Cleo's. I whispered a spell to calm them and assured them we would return soon.

While I did this my grandmother spoke the words over our red cloaks that would make us invisible until we landed our first strikes. We both had numerous blades strapped to our bodies that we hadn't removed to sleep, considering what we were hunting. She grabbed a short silver sword as well and quickly strapped it to her waist. I went for my favorite, a mahogany club that had been fitted with silver spikes, then dipped in silver so that it covered most of the dark wood except for the handle. It was how I spent my portion of the payment for our first hunt together.

Without a word we ran through the darkness. Since her vision was much better than mine, I followed her lead, trusting the path she sped along. Though I tried my best to imitate her, and she swore I did a good job, I had *never* seen anyone move the way my grandmother could. She was a force of nature and I could only aspire to her level.

My heart fluttered as excitement and trepidation coursed through me. Even I could smell the remnants of their campfire now. We were very close.

Shrieks of terror and curses rang in the night as we raced to hopefully save someone's life.

I was not prepared for the carnage that awaited us in that clearing. A large family had been traveling with a wagon. Bones crunched and someone beyond my sight screamed. The clearing echoed with the sounds of tearing flesh and the snarls of monsters. To our left a man was valiantly defending himself with a torch from a very large werewolf. To our right a child was crying as a woman was being torn to shreds before him.

My grandmother and I looked at each other before she went left and I went right.

The wolf turned to me, unable to see me until I made my first move, but still sensing something was not right. The woman's entrails spilled from his mouth and I realized with a growing sense of horror that she was still alive. She wailed pitifully as she tried to pull her insides from the creatures gaping jaws. There was nothing I could do to save her and it broke my heart. The monster turned suddenly and focused on the child. No! No! *No!* This was not happening. Not when I could stop it.

I leapt forward, swinging the club at the back of the crouching werewolf's head with every ounce of strength I possessed.

The child screamed as the monster bent closer, opening his jaws wide. My strike connected with his skull with a sickening crunch.

The beast howled and turned to face me, because now I was visible. I nearly threw up when I looked at him. The woman's insides were still hanging from his jaws as if they were stuck to his long teeth. I could hear her behind me choking on her own blood. I'd hit him so hard that one of his eyes had popped partially out of its socket.

He lifted his hand and with the back of his wrist pressed the eye back into place.

"You fucking cunt," he growled.

"Hide!" I yelled to the child.

The werewolf widened his feet, changing his stance as if he was about to pounce. Then he roared in my face so hard that drops of the woman's blood splashed against my cheeks.

I mimicked his stance, gripped my club tight and screamed right back at him, at the top of my lungs.

His laughter was a deep, terrifying rumble. "Oh, I'm going to enjoy this," he said.

"Come and get it, *cocksucker*!"

I began to move in an upward swing, turning my hips and putting all of my weight into the movement. I knew he was faster than me, so rather than wait for him to move, I anticipated what I thought he would do, just as Islene taught me.

I caught him right under the chin, clamping his jaws together so hard that he bit off part of his tongue.

The wolf howled and when he drew back I saw my opportunity. I dropped the club and pulled the knives strapped to my thighs. I hit the ground at a run, sliding between his legs. When I rolled to my feet behind him he turned quickly and laughed at me.

"What was that about?" he mocked. "Did you want a better look at my cock?"

It was then he realized he was bleeding. He put one clawed hand against his inner thigh and looked back to me in surprise.

"I've just cut the arteries in both your legs with silver. You won't heal before you bleed to death."

His roar of anger shook me to my core, but I held my ground and tried not to look afraid. On the inside though, I was pissing myself.

"I might be dead, bitch. But I will have you first," he growled.

He swung wide, claws out, but I was able to dodge. The blood loss was already slowing him down.

From the corner of my eye I saw my grandmother slice off the arm of the other werewolf as it leapt through the air. Her battle cry rang out as her red cloak flew past my line of sight.

I took a step back to avoid another swing and slipped in something. There was another dead man behind me and I'd just fallen in his still warm guts. I screamed as my hands slipped, trying to regain my footing.

The werewolf's laughter was vicious. "Have you never seen a man disemboweled before?" he growled. "Don't let it bother you too much. You'll be joining him before I die."

"Not tonight you piece of filth."

I grabbed one of the silver throwing knives from my belt and as he lunged at me again I hit him right in the eye.

He howled in agony and I rolled to the side, still in the poor man's entrails, but away from the gnashing jaws of the werewolf. As he fell to the ground I tore off toward my club. The wolf was by now significantly weakened from blood loss and as he rolled to his back I brought down the silver spikes as hard as I could into his face.

He reached for me and I narrowly avoided being scratched as I brought the weapon down again with another crunch. I screamed as I slammed the club into his face over and over again, like I was chopping wood.

I have seen people who were killed by werewolves before, but never witnessed the event taking place. The savagery of these kills was also beyond my realm of experience. The bodies I'd seen before this had their throats torn out or their stomachs torn open, but not disemboweled. One was missing a head. Their deaths had been fast. But these animals … they were tearing people apart for the sheer joy of it.

I was still screaming when I felt my grandmother's hand on my back.

"Bella, he's dead."

I stopped and gasped for air, leaning heavily on my club.

"You do realize we need to show the heads as proof of our kill, right?"

I laughed, then immediately felt sick again. "I can't believe I can laugh at a time like this."

"It's either that or cry," she said.

"There is a boy. I told him to hide. Did the man with the torch survive?"

She nodded to the corner of the clearing where the man was now curled up with his head against his knees, crying uncontrollably.

I turned to call for the boy and that's when the third werewolf walked out of the woods.

Chapter Eleven

Islene

With all the blood and the scent of fresh death around us I hadn't smelled him. That is my only excuse for not knowing there was a third werewolf.

Bella's face paled, but she stood her ground, taking a fighting stance as she lifted her club once more.

It was then I saw the wolf was holding someone out in front of him, like a shield.

"I come in peace." The man he held spoke, only it was the deep frightening voice of the wolf we heard.

"You wouldn't kill the messenger, would you?" he asked.

"That depends on the message," I called. "What have you got to say, monster?"

He laughed. "Monster? When I can smell the blood of The Beast in you?" he mocked.

The blood of The Beast? Who the fuck would know that?!

"Who are you?"

"As I said, I am only a messenger." Once again it was the man he held who spoke, but the wolf's voice we heard.

"If you keep repeating yourself I'm just going to cut your head off and be done. What have you got to say?"

"Look around you, whore, *this* is the message. I know who you are and he is coming for you. He's going to swallow you whole, red cloaks and all." He said all of this in a strange sing-song type of way.

Then he suddenly pulled his bloody hand out of the man in front of him. The werewolf waved his blood-covered fingers at us and said, "They don't make people like they used to, eh?"

I felt a scream building inside me as I realized he'd been using the man's body like a puppet.

Bella's scream was filled with rage as she stared the monster down.

"Does that make you angry, little hunter?" he asked, taking a step toward us. "Maybe after I kill you, I'll wrap your pretty red hair around my fist and fuck your face until my cock breaks through the back of your skull."

"Or maybe you should just shut up and die," she said.

Faster than I'd expected she threw two of the knives from her belt, both hitting him in the chest. The silver penetrated deeply and when he staggered back we both leapt upon him.

He shoved Bella aside but in the time he was focused on her I used my sword to chop off his right foot. He leapt toward me on one foot, continuing to hop as I dodged backwards. He swung at me twice before I ducked underneath his arm, stabbing upward through his rib cage and directly into his heart.

The monster choked on blood and grabbed the silver sword, but to no avail. He was fading fast. I grabbed his head, forcing him to look me in the eye.

"Who are you?" I hissed. "How do you know about me?"

As the light faded from his eyes he laughed, spilling blood onto my hands. "He's not dead, bitch," he coughed.

I could only stare in horror as the werewolf died. Surely he didn't mean Bastian was still alive?

Chapter Twelve

Belladonna

Dawn broke over the horizon as my grandmother and I helped to load the last of the family's remains into the wagon. It felt so macabre, placing the corpses beside their possessions in the narrow space.

The bodies of the werewolves were nearly finished burning. We built up what remained of the family's campfire and used it to help clean up the area as best we could. Since this was a fairly well-traveled route, we thought it best to not leave the werewolves for the other creatures of the forest to dispose of.

The man and boy we'd saved were father and son. The woman I was not fast enough to protect was the boy's mother. We wrapped the bodies as best we could in sheets and some of their cloaks, to spare the child and his father from having to continue to look at what was left of their loved ones in such a state.

They'd been traveling to Viande and were going to follow us back.

"I've scouted the area," my grandmother said to me. "I don't smell anything else out here besides some deer and a few, likely very confused, pheasants."

I'd gathered the three massive werewolf heads into sacks that were now tied to the back of her horse. Not all who hired us required proof of the job being completed in this way, but some did. I vomited twice in the bushes.

I took the water skin from the bag on Samson and rinsed my mouth for the second time.

"At least we didn't have to travel as far as we'd thought," I said. "Unless I'm mistaken, the location the crystal pointed to is another full day's ride from here." I sighed. "It's good that we are finished already, but bad they were so close to home."

I glanced back and realized she wasn't even listening to me. She was completely lost in her own thoughts.

"What he said," she whispered. "It isn't possible."

"About The Beast?"

"Shhh, keep your voice down. Yes. I *know* he wasn't breathing." To my surprise she began to cry. "I checked several times for a heartbeat. I buried him myself. Bastian Cheney was *dead*. Even after all he'd done, I could not have buried him alive."

She put a hand over her heart as if it ached. In that moment the pieces fell into place and I understood the one detail my grandmother left out of her story.

"You loved him," I said softly. When she looked surprised I explained, "I can see it in your eyes when you said his name."

"If anyone ever found out—"

"They won't. Not from me, not ever."

She hugged me tightly, then pulled back and wiped the smeared kohl underneath her eyes.

"Only Royce knows and I just told him yesterday."

"I understand now, why you never bragged about killing a legendary werewolf. Why it seemed to cause you pain to discuss it rather than joy at putting an end to a monster. The sadness behind your eyes when anyone was happy to meet you because of what you'd done. It all makes perfect sense now." I squeezed her hand gently. "I am so sorry, grandmother."

Her eyes glistened with tears again. "When did you become so insightful?"

"He was the one who bit you?"

"Yes."

"And you think that's who this deranged creature was talking about?"

"Reasonably, he couldn't possibly be talking about Bastian. But what he said—"

"Was meant to upset you by someone who must know the truth."

She shook her head. "Until yesterday, I hadn't breathed a word of this in thirty four years, not to a soul."

"Was anyone else there? Did he have any friends or family who could have known?"

"He had a brother, Gaston, but I don't believe he knew what had become of Bastian until after his death. Unfortunately, at some point he also became a werewolf. I didn't know this until after Maroc told me the name of the last werewolf he killed. I'm sure there is more than one Gaston Cheney in the world, but we both believed him to be Bastian's brother."

"Are you telling me that the brother of The Beast is the one who killed your friend, Maroc's father?"

She nodded. "We didn't realize this until after the fact. Had I know, maybe I would have gone on that last hunt. I'm not sure. Either way, I never met him. Bastian only mentioned him once and that was to say he was his only living relative and he was currently in Moldavia. No one knows about what I am except for you and Royce. I never told anyone I was bitten, let alone by *him*."

"Then maybe the wolf was lying. Maybe he wanted to say something horrible to you with his last breath because he knew he couldn't kill you."

She sighed. "That is a good possibility, given his obvious capacity for evil."

"Since you can smell the difference in them, is it so hard to believe they can do the same with you? Even if you didn't change, you probably don't smell like I do."

"We used the oil to cover our scents."

"And we sweated and fought and it probably wore off, at least partially."

She seemed to consider my words for a moment. "I *don't* smell like everyone else," she said at last. "Maybe the blood of The Beast was an expression referring to all werewolves? While they are all beasts, only one was ever so terrible that he was known as *The* Beast."

"I believe he could smell the difference in you and he said what he did because *he was a monster*. End of story."

She nodded and seemed to feel better, at least her expression brightened.

During this conversation the man and his son had gone to the nearby stream to wash the blood from their hair and change clothes. Just then they walked back into sight and she nodded at me as if to confirm we would not speak of this near them.

"I don't believe I thanked you," the man said softly as he came to stand beside us.

My unkind words about the villagers came back to haunt me and I felt ashamed. Tears stung my eyes, realizing the horror of what this man had been through. Though I didn't witness the murder of my parents by werewolves, I certainly understood his grief. As a child I often lay awake at night, wondering exactly how my parents had met their end. Finally, Islene started to give me some tea she brewed to help me sleep.

"You will drive yourself mad with wondering, child," she'd told me. "You must make yourself stop so that you can live." She was right.

"There is no need," I said to him, my throat tight with emotion. "I am only sorry I couldn't save your wife."

The boy reached out and took my hand. His face was still flushed and his eyes were rimmed red from crying.

"You saved me," he said.

"And you saved me," the man said to my grandmother. "My name is Angus, and this is Henri. Can I ask you a question?"

I nodded as my grandmother answered, "Of course."

He looked to the fire that was barely more than ashes and a few bones now. My grandmother added a potion when he wasn't looking, to make the fire burn hot enough to consume the bodies.

"Why did they remain monstrous? I've always heard that when a werewolf is killed, they turn back into the person they once were."

"Some do. I believe it depends on whether they have the strength left at the moment of death for a transformation. I've seen werewolves who used their last bit of life to transform back into their human form, to try to spare their loved ones knowing what they were. I know that to change back from their wolf form leaves them significantly weakened, especially if they are not strong to begin with. Often, in a fight to the death, what you saw is how werewolves appear, even after death."

The man nodded slowly. "I never thought about it that way before."

He seemed dazed, no doubt from all he had seen. My grandmother put a hand on his shoulder and said, "Try *not* to think about it. And when we reach Viande, I will bring you something to help you rest, as soon as I can.

That is, if you will accept some herbal tea from a strange apothecary whom you just met."

"Gladly," he said. "Is it safe for Henri as well?"

She nodded as I told him, "I took it as a child. Though I did not witness it, my parents were also killed by werewolves. The tea stopped my nightmares."

Tears filled his eyes. Angus seemed unable to speak and simply nodded his approval before turning to their wagon. Moments later he and Henri were both up front in the coachman's seat. Miraculously, their two horses were unharmed.

"What now?" I asked as I climbed onto Samson's back.

"We take them back with us, help them find where they need to go, and take these heads to the mayor. I'm sure he'll want them displayed on spikes outside of town. If your wolf was correct, we're still missing one. He must be the alpha."

"We'll find him," I assured her.

"First we will recover and think about our next move. I will reinforce the protections on our home and around the forest, and then yes, we will find the bastard and end this."

Chapter Thirteen

Wolf

She was out there somewhere, my little red. I could feel her. How that was possible, I had no idea. I had wondered since meeting her if she'd bewitched me somehow. Did I care if she had? Not particularly.

I had no desire to deceive her, fate had determined that she meet my bestial side first. If any woman would ever be with me, she needed to know me. All of me. That was always my intention ... but I was not ready to show her my other side. Not yet. Considering our circumstances I don't know if that made me a coward or simply cautious.

I walked out into the woods before I let the change take me. I held up the oversized trousers as I trudged forward, barefoot. No sense in ruining perfectly good shoes. I smiled as I recalled her asking me why I wore trousers. I'm not sure why I didn't tell her the real reason. I didn't want my cock flapping around in a fight. I could understand why females who turned didn't bother with clothes. Everything they had was concealed by fur.

I looked up at the moon with a sigh. It was nowhere near full, though that was not the only cause for a werewolf to transform, as many learned too late. Once they learn how, a werewolf can change their skin as easily as changing clothes. Alphas can do this more often in a shorter amount of time than a wolf of lesser abilities. There are some who never learn control and only change during the height of the lunar cycle, and others who lose control entirely and remain a wolf until their life is ended.

Very soon after becoming what I am, I learned I could not only change at will, but I can change one part of my body and not another. I used to practice growing only my claws. The height of the full moon is the only time that we *must* transform. I have never found any literature nor heard any tales that define exactly why this is. Though it isn't from lack of trying. I've uncovered many interesting books about werewolves over the last five years, far beyond the reach of what most have heard, even hunters.

The transformation ceased to cause me true pain after the first few times. However, that did not mean it wasn't thoroughly unpleasant.

I clenched my fists as the bones in my hands cracked and began to reform. I opened my arms wide and stretched, arching my back as my spine popped, bent, and then lengthened.

I wriggled my toes as claws extended from my newly reformed feet, sinking into the earth. I hadn't realized I was standing under such low limbs until my height increased slightly and I was poked in the ear. Thank goodness being overly tall was not a feature often looked for in the human forms of those suspected of being a werewolf. My height is the biggest reason for my anxiousness at having Bella see me in my other skin. I am head and shoulders taller than the majority of men I've met, making me an even larger werewolf. Eventually, she will *have* to see me as a man. When she does, I wonder if she will know my secret immediately, or if will it take her some time to be certain. Or will it be my scent that gives me away? Any other woman would never notice such a thing, other than to note my appealing fragrance. But Bella is not any other woman. She is aware of the allure an alpha male can possess. How long could she be in my presence as a man and not realize the truth?

I've even read that some cultures, like the Japanese, consider women to be the best at hunting werewolves. Not necessarily due to any extra prowess in fighting, but because they are more likely to listen to how their bodies respond. In this way they can most easily detect a werewolf, even when they still look like an ordinary man or woman.

This is another aspect of my animal nature that I had yet to find an explanation for. The best answer I'd found was from an old Chinese scroll that I had translated. It described the scent of a werewolf to be nearly impossible to resist if they were in a state of arousal. In the case of alpha wolves, arousal isn't necessary to find *both* sexes drawn to you. If one knows how to wield such power, being a werewolf in secret can be a powerful weapon against both enemies and allies.

I've found men more easily persuaded to my point of view, even if upon being questioned by someone else later, they disagree with me. When in my presence, I can win them over. Has Bella ever been around another werewolf enough to know this about them and will it cause her to know me for what I am?

What will I say then? How will I tell her who I am and why I've kept this secret from her?

Perhaps on some level she *does* know and fate will play things out as it must.

I moved farther into the cover of the trees and tried to clear my thoughts. My mind needed to be on the hunt and nothing else.

While out riding with Claude this morning I caught a scent that chilled me to the bone. Claude is not only my valet, but my friend. He is the only one who knows. After the second pair of overly large trousers turned up in shreds he became suspicious. He is not old enough to be my father, but still he practically raised me and could tell something was amiss since my father's death. I took him into my confidence soon afterward and he has been helping me cover my tracks ever since.

I tried to hide my reaction from him when I caught the scent, not wanting to give him further cause for concern. I forced myself to sound calm as I left, telling him I was looking for the rest of the pack I'd tracked. However, that scent was not merely another werewolf, but one I thought had been dead for five years. I hoped tonight's hunt would prove me wrong. Though I had yet to know of my senses being wrong since becoming a wolf, I truly hoped I was mistaken this time.

I crouched low and began to run through the woods on all fours. The ground came up fast to meet my palms as I felt the cool damp grass crunch beneath my hands. Freedom. That's what it felt like to let the beast out for a run. Complete freedom.

The cold night wind wiped through my fur, bringing with it the scent of another werewolf. It was a female and she was close. I recognized her scent as part of the pack I'd discovered recently. I paused, taking another deep breath. Her smell was mingled with traces of human blood.

She was definitely one of the killers on the loose.

I ran faster, keeping my nose near the ground. A soft rain was beginning to fall and I didn't want to lose her scent. I was close to a stream and at first the sounds of the water trickling past almost drowned out the screams. Almost.

I lifted up from all fours, widening my stride in the hopes that I could find someone still alive.

Suddenly a man hit me full in the chest. He was running nearly as hard as I was, but since I was much bigger, he bounced off of me and hit the ground. It only took him a moment to catch his breath enough to scream.

"*Putain de merde*! There are two of them!" Another scream tore from his throat as I slapped my hand over his mouth.

"Will you shut the fuck up," I growled.

His eyes went wide and he tried to struggle against my hand.

"I'm trying very hard not to scratch you," I said calmly. "I am here to help. I know how that must sound to you, but if you stop squirming and point me in the right direction, I will kill the bitch that's after you."

He nodded tightly and ceased to fight. When I removed my hand his first words were, "The cunt is right behind me. She's probably already eaten my friend. Bitch nearly bit my cock off."

I shook my head and held up a hand. "I don't need the details." I looked at him again to see if he was obviously bitten or deeply scratched anywhere. "Why are you naked?"

"I thought you didn't need the details," he quipped.

"You know what, you're right. I don't. I am curious though."

On that note I ran in the direction he'd indicated, leapt across the small stream and followed the sounds of a second man screaming. The first thing I saw as I entered the clearing was a woman's back turned to me.

She was half transformed and what little remained of her clothes hung in shreds of dark green. Her long ebony hair was wild and trailed in the wind, swirling around her like the storm.

There was a half-naked man in a tree in front of her, looking down on the scene with such horror that I pitied him. His face clearly said that if he survived this night he might never sleep again.

I heard a sickening crunch and realized there had been a fourth person in the clearing. I stepped toward her with a growl.

"What do you think you are doing in my territory?"

"*Your* territory?"

She rose to her full height and turned to me. The dead man was clearly visible now by her feet and his heart was in her hand.

"That's right. These people are mine to protect, not yours to eat and terrorize."

She threw back her head and laughed as her face grew longer and more lupine though didn't quite finish transforming. She was showing me her power by holding her form somewhere in between. I was not concerned.

"What kind of werewolf protects humans?" She sneered and took a bite of the heart. Blood gushed and poured down her arm. Steam rose from the warm heart in her hand, much like my breath began to fog on the cold night air.

Before she could chew I backhanded her so hard she fell, stumbling over the dead man. The heart fell from her hand and she nearly choked on the piece in her mouth as she fought to regain her footing.

"You've picked the wrong fight, *idiot*," she growled.

I snarled and braced for her attack. "Is that the best you've got, *idiot*? I was thinking of calling you a filthy hag, at the very least."

"You toy with me, fool?"

"You do realize that idiot and fool are basically the same thing?"

She roared with obvious frustration and rage. "I am the delta wolf of our pack!"

"And I am the alpha wolf of this territory, *cunt*."

"Cunt? That's the best you've got, *mon homme*? Filthy hag was much better." This came from the man up in the tree.

"Fine, you do the insulting and I'll do the fighting," I said with a growl.

She glanced over her shoulder and gave the man a low snarl. "No one asked you, meat."

She turned back to me suddenly, but when she leapt I was ready. I sidestepped quickly and using my longer reach to my advantage, I ran my claws down her back.

She screamed and dropped to all fours, completing her transformation in seconds. When she lashed out again I was unprepared for how much faster she'd become. Her teeth sank deeply into my thigh. I punched the side of her head twice before her jaws released me.

"Mmmm, I like the way you taste," she purred, licking her lips.

"That's what she said before she ate Pierre," the man in the tree yelled.

"You're not helping!"

The she-wolf laughed and wiped her mouth with the back of one clawed hand. "I'm going to enjoy devouring you."

When she came at me again I was ready. I ducked low as she flew at my head with all her strength, probably meaning to decapitate me. As I dropped to the grass I slashed the underside of her body.

She fell to the ground, writhing and screaming, a string of curses falling from her fanged mouth.

When she stood up I realized what I'd done and immediately felt sick. It's not that I haven't seen and done my share of violence. I still have a deep rooted aversion to harming a woman, even one who is trying to kill me.

"Do you see what you've done to me, *sale merde*?!"

"I take back everything I ever thought about female werewolves. You should really consider wearing clothes to fight."

"Gaston will never fuck me now!" she roared. "Who wants to fuck a she-wolf with one tit?"

I almost laughed. "It will grow back, if you survive. You might still do that by telling me where to find your alpha."

She spit blood on the ground just in front of my feet.

"I'll take that as a no." I gestured back to the dead man. "I'm going to guess *he* isn't Gaston, because that poor man won't be fucking anyone unless it's in Hell."

I tried to not show any further reaction to the name. It couldn't be him. That bastard was missing a head when last I saw him. Then I remembered that lingering trace of a scent from this morning. Could another wolf smell so much like him? Perhaps someone he turned before his death? Oh, *mon Dieu* … did I carry a trace of his scent as well?

"*Will* it? I've never had a tit ripped off by another wolf before. And I believe you know who I'm talking about. I can see it in your eyes."

I put as much menace into my already deepened voice as possible as I said, "Tell me where to find him and you can go."

I left out the part that if I didn't catch her later, Bella or Islene surely would if she stayed around here very long.

"The only way you will get near my alpha is if I drag your corpse back in the hopes of a reward."

She launched herself at me with a ferocity I'd rarely seen. She became a blur of fangs, fur, and claws. *Merde*, she was fast.

After she clawed her way down my back and bit my right arm, I got past my aversion to causing her further grievous harm.

When she lunged forward for another attack I grabbed her by the throat and slammed her to the ground. The rain fell harder, splashing around us as I knelt over her, still squeezing my claws into her neck.

"What if I told you they tried to rape me," she gasped.

I hesitated causing my grip to loosen just a bit. I was rewarded with her claws sinking deeply into my ribs. She thrust her body upward beneath me, wrapping her legs around my waist as she rolled us over, taking me to the ground this time.

"Fool," she laughed. "It is *I* who does the raping around here! Men are so simple, and always ready to take their clothes off with a beautiful woman. I was going to rip off their cocks and stuff them up each other's arses. Can you imagine what would be said about them when their bodies were found?"

The entire time she talked the she-wolf kept throwing open handed strikes to my ribs. I protected my face as she gouged me down both sides, repeatedly.

Enough of this. She was fast and I was losing too much blood. I bucked my hips upward, throwing her off of me. When she leapt toward me I punched her with all my strength.

My hand went straight through her chest and came out her back, holding her still beating heart.

She looked down at the arm that penetrated her body with a mixture of shock and horror.

"I only hesitated so long because I don't enjoy hurting women," I explained.

She laughed and blood gushed from her mouth. "It bothers you," she wheezed. "Then I will make you see the full horror of what you've done."

As I withdrew my arm from her body she used the last of her strength to turn back into a woman. Somewhere during our final struggle the rain had stopped.

With her heart still in my hand, I looked down at her and ate it in one big bite.

I could feel my injuries already beginning to heal as I whipped out my cock and pissed on her corpse.

I hadn't realized that both surviving men were now watching me until one of them asked, "Is that really necessary?"

I laughed and stuffed myself back into my trousers. I don't think either of them needed to see a big fat wolf cock after the night they'd already had.

"Her alpha will find her this way. This *is* my territory and I am marking it as such."

The naked man I'd run into earlier was now scrambling to gather his clothes from around the campsite. He looked up at his friend who was still in the tree. "Are you coming down?"

"That depends on whether or not he's still hungry."

I laughed again. "I ate her heart to help heal my injuries, not because of hunger. If I wanted to eat either of you, I would have already. I am sorry about your other friend though."

"We barely knew him," the man said, swinging down from the tree with the lithe grace of a dancer. "He joined us at the last tavern."

"We will see that he is buried with respect," the other man answered as he laced his breeches. "Thank you. You saved our lives."

He seemed thoroughly puzzled by this.

"Just because I look like a monster, doesn't mean I am one."

"*Merci*," the second man said. "I am Jacque, this is Peter. That poor dead oaf is Pierre. We were just passing through."

"Well, gentlemen, I suggest you continue on your way. She is not the last werewolf roaming these woods with the intent to do harm."

"You don't have to tell me twice," Peter said, pulling on his boots. "After we bury Pierre, I'm getting the *fuck* out of these woods and back onto the main road. I'm not stopping until I reach the next village."

"Good plan," I agreed. "But there may not be time for you to bury your friend. I'm not certain how close the rest of her pack might be.

I'll see to his remains, if that's all right with you."

"Yes, and thank you again."

"I can't believe I'm talking to a werewolf," Jacque said, still keeping his distance.

"*That* is your concern after what just happened?" Peter said. He threw a tunic and travel bag at his companion. "Let's go before he decides he *is* hungry after all."

They circled the campsite, roughly stuffing the rest of their wet belongings into two bags before taking off at a trot through the woods.

I wrapped Pierre in what remained of his clothing and carried him far enough away from the dead she-wolf that I believed his remains would be left alone. I rested him against the roots of a tree before using my big hands and claws to dig a shallow grave.

"I am sorry," I said to him. "I don't know if you had anyone I should return you to. If your companions knew, they chose not to say. This should keep you from being found by the pack, when they find the she-wolf. At least your body will not be further desecrated. If I ever hear anyone looking for a man named Pierre who meets your description, I will make certain they know where to find you."

I grabbed handfuls of large rocks from the riverbed nearby until his grave was covered completely. Mist had settled over the land as I looked out across the forest from the hill.

"As far as final resting places go, you could do worse." I placed the final rock letting my palm rest against the stone. "May you find peace in death, and safer travels."

Chapter Fourteen

Wolf

I had purposely avoided going toward the area I knew Bella and Islene would be hunting. How did I know where they'd go? Because I was once a hunter and *I* would go to the last location where I knew someone was killed by a werewolf. I could not be certain they hadn't encountered a situation similar to what I saw tonight. But if they had not, the last murder to be discussed in the village was that of a woman, not far from here.

If this is the trail they chose to follow, that would take them to the outskirts of Pomme de Terre. I had stayed in the large forests that surround Viande. I had every confidence in their abilities, and I didn't want to catch a silver arrow to the chest, or a crossbow bolt tipped with wolfsbane. But now ... I needed to find her, to see her. I needed to know she still lived.

I didn't give myself time to think about it, I simply took off running through the woods. I knew this area better than any map and could travel even faster than a horse in my animal form.

I ran for more than an hour before I caught the scent of woodsmoke mingled with flesh. Someone was either cooking or burning bodies. The sun rose as I took another deep breath and followed the scent. Another half hour of running and I found the remains of a large campsite. The fire was nearly out. I sniffed again. Though the air was heavy with the scent of rain the ground here was dry. I'd outrun the storm. It would be here soon.

I picked up a stick and poked the ashes. A few large bone fragments remained. Definitely burning bodies.

I looked around more closely. Dark red patches stained the ground. I didn't need a closer look to know it was blood. There were wagon tracks and signs of a struggle. Deep gouges marked the ground in several places, both from claws and other weapons.

I took a few steps and saw that tiny pieces of bone were splintered in a circular pattern amidst a large pool of blood that had yet to be fully absorbed by the earth.

More blood and obvious signs of fighting were scattered about as well as a few tufts of fur. One sniff told me the fur belonged to werewolves.

I left the clearing and ran along the road, keeping hidden just off the main trail. When I heard the sounds of horses and a wagon I slowed my pace. Bella and Islene were clearly leading people back to Viande. The smell let me know the poor people were carrying their dead with them.

When I saw her there on her horse, looking well, I breathed a heavy sigh of relief. Her long red hair had started to come loose from her braid as wavy tendrils drifted in the wind. Kohl was smeared underneath her eyes in a way that looked as though she'd been crying. She looked fierce. I had never witnessed a more beautiful sight in my life.

I almost ran to her, which was the stupidest thing I could possibly do under the circumstances. Thankfully, I stopped myself.

I couldn't let her see me like this. She only knew me as a werewolf so far, but I was covered in blood, parts of my fur were matted with it despite running through the rain. I smelled of death and a bit like a wet dog. Not to mention I didn't want to further upset the survivors. God only knows what they'd already been through, without some idiotic werewolf running out of the woods, yelling the name of one of their saviors.

Islene and I had met before, but would she know me like this? I hoped not. Still, I remained hidden. Bella was alive and heading back to the safety of home. That was enough for me, for now.

I looked down at my body as thoughts ran quickly through my mind. I wanted to see her today, to talk to her. But she only knew this form. I could not simply show up as a strange man on her doorstep without an explanation I wasn't yet sure how to give. This meant I needed to shift back, bathe, and then become a werewolf once again before seeing Bella.

Normally this was not an issue for me. I could shift my form up to four times a day if necessary without needing to rest. But after the night I'd had, if I turned back now I would need a nap. The longer I could stay in this form, the faster my injuries would heal. I lost far too much blood and had to allow my body to recover. This would also take a lot of energy, making my exhaustion even greater when I finally shifted back to a man. There wasn't time to sleep. At least, that is the way I felt.

"I'll bathe like this," I said to myself as I turned and ran away. "If Claude comes into my chambers, it certainly won't be the strangest thing he's ever seen me do."

Chapter Fifteen

Belladonna

That afternoon, after we settled our business in town, and my grandmother had finished reinforcing the protection wards, I went out to hunt. I was hunting deer this time, not werewolves. We are all very fortunate that the d'Ulfric's do not place hunting restrictions on the people who live here. Poaching fines remain in some parts of the country if anything larger than a rabbit is killed.

My grandmother's usual routine was to go visit Royce Severin after a hunt. She said that talking to him helped to clear her mind. Royce is a very handsome man and I'm sure he is a great *conversationalist.* That's where she was when I made my way deep into the woods in the opposite direction.

Before leaving town I kept the promise my grandmother made. I sent a message to Comte Maroc d'Ulfric, letting him know our hunt was a success and I was ready to formalize our agreement. That was hours ago. The messenger had likely reached him by now. I wondered if Maroc was happy to hear from me or did he have second thoughts as well and was simply honoring his father's agreement.

~ 123 ~

My mind said I was doing the right thing, keeping my word. But my heart wanted to see Wolf. Still, I did not bring the strip of cloth with his blood into the woods with me. I didn't want his scent to accidentally frighten away game. I did, however, bring the pouch with the long silver chain; I'm not sure why.

I was sitting on a low branch in an oak tree, watching a large buck. I moved slowly as I lifted my bow and took aim. I had helped hunt for our meals since I was a child and was very good at it. I didn't take pleasure in killing, but I did enjoy the feeling of accomplishment at being able to contribute. I carried a sack with me. The buck would never fit, of course, but I could use it to help me drag him back to the sled I used for larger game. Not knowing what I might find, I'd left the sled a ways back just as a precaution. As I assessed the buck once more I realized he was at the limit of what I would be able to carry back on my own.

Even as I took aim and tried to steady my breathing, my heart was beating too fast, because my thoughts kept returning to Wolf.

"There you are."

I gasped at the sound of his deep voice behind me. Not only did my arrow miss, scaring away the deer, I fell out of the tree. I tumbled forward off the branch and right into the waiting arms of the biggest werewolf I'd ever seen.

He held me tightly against his broad chest and when I breathed in his familiar scent, I knew there was nowhere else I'd rather be. There was something a bit different about the way he smelled this time. I pressed my face against his fur and breathed him in.

"Why do you smell like soap?"

"Because I bathed."

My mind was filled with images of a massive werewolf hanging over the edges of a tub, covered in suds. I laughed.

"You mean to tell me that you bathed like *this* and washed all of your fur?"

"Is that so strange?"

"It is when you could turn back into a man rather than lather up all this hair."

"I have my reasons."

"You scared away my deer."

"I see your other hunt was successful," he said. "I've always felt that displaying heads on the outskirts of villages was a bit disgusting."

I laughed softly. "That is strange, coming from a creature designed for bloodshed."

"What happened to that *one*? It was nearly beaten into porridge."

I almost gagged with the memory. "I beat him to death with a club."

He looked down at me and his already large amber eyes widened with surprise. "*You* did that?"

"I'm not proud of it, but believe me when I say he deserved every strike."

"I ran through the clearing where I'm certain they met their end, judging by all the blood. It looked like a massacre."

I closed my eyes for a moment, trying *not* to see the faces of the dead. "It was, but not only of werewolves."

"I'm sorry," he said softly. "Were you or your grandmother harmed?"

"No." I paused for a moment and realized how good it felt to put my hand against his chest. I let it rest there, palm flat, feeling his heartbeat. "I didn't summon you, Wolf."

His laughter was a deep, sensual caress. "And yet here you are in my arms, making no effort to escape."

"I'm not afraid of you." I looked up at his long wolf face and felt the truth of my words. "I see you, and you look similar to the monsters we fought last night, but you are *nothing* alike. Everything about you *feels* different."

"That's because I *am* different. You may not have used my blood to signal me, but you reached out nonetheless. I felt your call."

Did I bring him here with my thoughts, with the force of my longing?

Before I could comment on what he'd just said he continued, "There is something I should tell you. I was on a hunt of my own last night. I found the fourth wolf."

"Well, that's wonderful news, isn't it? The threat to this area has ended."

"Not quite."

"But you did kill him, didn't you?"

"I did. *She* was strong, but not an alpha."

"She? From what one of them said to us, we thought the last werewolf was a male. Or perhaps the wolf last night was lying to scare us, just like we suspected."

"And is a male inherently more frightening?" His tone was playful and somehow arousing to me.

"Not unless you're afraid of cock, I suppose. It wasn't necessarily the sex of the werewolf, but the things that were said about him." I forced myself to stop talking before I said too much.

"Unfortunately, I don't think she was the last werewolf in this area. The she-wolf mentioned a pack, of which she claimed to be the third strongest. Werewolves would not gather like this without an alpha to follow. Whoever is still out there, I'm afraid they are very dangerous. If you and your grandmother agree, I would like to join you on your next hunt."

I was stunned and not entirely sure what my grandmother would say about a werewolf wanting to join us. "Why?"

"Because I want to help, and to protect you from whatever monsters have entered my territory."

"*Your* territory? Are you saying that *you* are the biggest baddest wolf around here?"

"*Chérie*, I am *the* big bad wolf. And yes, this is my territory." He lowered me down gently, making sure to rub my body down the front of his. "Everything you see here is *mine*."

"Is that how you feel about women you find in the woods?"

With one large claw he tilted my chin up to look at him. "Only one," he said softly. "My only regret with this form is that I cannot kiss you properly."

"You kissed me just fine the last time," I teased.

"Ah, but a different set of lips." He growled and ran his long tongue over his fangs. "I was hoping for something *more* this time, though I did enjoy the way you taste."

"To my knowledge I have never been with a man who was a werewolf, let alone fucked one in their wolfman form."

I was amazed that the face of a monster could show so much expression.

"Oh, so now you're fucking me?"

I reached up and put my hand flat against his rigid abdomen, pushing him back playfully.

"I'm thinking about it."

"Mmmmm," he growled. The sound sent a thrill through me.

He closed the distance between us and when I looked at him this time, towering over me, body to body, the full enormity of his size was frightening. My voice was a breathy whisper as I asked, "How big is your cock?"

My heart felt like it was trying to leap from my chest at simply voicing the question.

He looked down at me with an expression I could only describe as hunger. Such a masculine look, even on an animal's face.

"Are you afraid you can't take me, little red?" his deep voice rumbled.

I reached out and stroked the front of his tight trousers.

His hiss of pleasure made me shiver with excitement.

"I am nothing if not bold," I said. I pressed my hand more firmly against his growing length and gasped. "What a big cock you have, Wolf."

"The better to make you scream," he growled. "Are you going to simply stand there stroking it, torturing me?"

"I'm trying to assess my odds of surviving without serious injury if I try to ride it."

His deep laughter was pure sin, carnal, wanton, and utterly inviting.

"In the time it takes to wonder, you could know," he purred.

I stroked him again and was surprised when I was the one to moan with pleasure.

"This is the biggest cock I've ever touched."

"Ah, but you have yet to actually touch it," he teased.

"Would you like me to?"

His grin was devilish. "You know I would."

I quickly opened his trousers, but paused before touching him. "My hands are cold," I explained.

He laughed softly. "Warm them on me."

I put my palm flat against his abdomen, letting his warmth seep into my cool skin as I listened to the sound of his breathing. Once again I was given pause by the sheer size of him. His waist was level with my shoulders, putting his now open trousers almost directly in front of my face.

He growled softly as I ran my hand down lower. I was enjoying the feel of his soft fur and hard muscles and savoring the delicious anticipation.

"Go on," he beckoned, "touch it."

I trembled slightly as I reached in and wrapped my hand around his incredibly thick shaft.

"Oh," I gasped.

"Take it out," he purred.

I did as he asked and freed his enormous member from his clothing. For a moment all I could do was stand there and stare as I stroked him. I had seen other werewolves' cocks before, because I'd never met another who wore clothing. Theirs were either so small they'd been hidden by longer fur, or they were very hairy.

Wolf was nothing like what I'd seen before. I needed both hands to hold it all. His flesh was warm and smooth, not covered in fur as I'd expected, but much more like a normal man. At least in appearance. Size was another matter.

"What do you think?" he asked. "Do you think you can take it?"

My heart was hammering away like a deranged blacksmith who'd had too much to drink.

"I am both excited and completely terrified at the thought of putting this inside of me."

His deep sensual laughter resonated within my chest and caused my pussy to ache with need.

"I understand if you're intimidated by the size, but never be afraid of me," he said. "If you want me, I am yours. If you are afraid, we can find other ways to enjoy one another."

I took a step back and reached for the pouch on my belt. "You are mine?"

He opened his arms wide in invitation. The curve of his hips was magnificent and clearly visible as his fur was much thinner along his chest and abdomen, giving a view of his perfectly sculpted muscles. He just stood there, trousers open, cock out, arms spread wide.

"Do with me as you wish, little red."

"I think I will." The thin silver chain glinted in the light shining through the trees as I pulled it from my pouch. "I have no desire to hurt you," I explained. "I only want to be certain that *I* am in control. Is this agreeable for you?"

He nodded slowly. "It *will* hurt, but I like a bit of pain sometimes." He thrust his hips at me. "And I hope you do as well."

My sex clenched in response. "Sit down," I instructed. "Put your back against that tree."

"Should I take these off first?" he asked, gesturing to his trousers.

I looked him up and down again. "Can you get them over your feet?"

He laughed and slid his trousers to mid-thigh instead. When he did this he bent over right in front of me, giving me a display of his round muscular arse.

He sat down and flashed his teeth in what I knew was a smile but to anyone else may have appeared to be a threat. "Shall I put my hands behind me?"

"Yes."

I approached him slowly. He was still very imposing, even like this. I had to get close to do what I needed to do. As I wrapped the silver chain across his chest he growled softly in my ear causing me to shiver again. I moved behind the tree and secured his wrists.

I walked back around the tree and straddled one of his outstretched legs.

"Comfortable?" I asked.

"Do we really need the chain?"

"Have you ever been with a woman in your werewolf form before?"

"No. And you said you've never been with a man like me."

"You could always turn back and show me your human side."

"That wouldn't make my cock any smaller."

I laughed, but I was also very curious to know if this was boasting or true.

"I'm not ready for you to know that part of me, yet. Besides, transforming would use a lot of my strength, leaving me vulnerable and still a good distance from my home."

Suddenly I understood. "That's why you washed all of your fur rather than turning back. You didn't want to be too tired to find me."

"And fuck you," he corrected. "You shouldn't leave out the best part."

"We shall see if that's the best part." I began to loosen my corset and smiled when this brought a low growl from his lips. "Are you truly restrained or pretending for my benefit?"

"You'll have to trust me," he said. "How else can you let me inside you?"

I tossed my cloak underneath the tree beside him and my corset and knives quickly followed. He watched hungrily while I slid off my boots and leggings. I stood there for a moment with nothing between us but my tunic. He seemed confused when I slid my boots back on. "My feet are cold," I explained.

The cold breeze was a shock against my wet pussy as I once again moved to stand over him, legs wide.

"What will you do with me now?" he asked.

Was such a magnificent beast truly my prisoner or did he merely choose to be?

I bumped my foot against his thigh. "Put your legs closer together." When he did this I straddled his legs just above the knee.

I smiled as I took his giant cock into my hands once more. "You're not even fully hard yet."

"I can change the size if you like," he offered.

"You can ... *what*?"

He laughed and I ran one hand between my legs to stroke my clit. This brought his laughter to an abrupt halt and made me smile again.

~ 135 ~

I was still sitting on his legs as I spread my thighs wider, opening myself completely to his view. I pulled my tunic up higher, giving him an unencumbered look at exactly what I was doing to myself.

"Oh," he said as I reached out to touch him with one hand.

"You were saying?"

"I can change the size of my cock, just as I can make my claws grow and nothing else. I know I can make it larger, because I have before. But if you don't think you can take it as it is, I can try to make it smaller."

"Don't you dare." I took the hand I'd been using to stroke my pussy and used it to rub some of my wetness up and down his shaft. "This is the most magnificent piece of meat I've ever seen and I won't stop until I stuff it inside of me."

"You have such a wonderfully filthy mouth," he growled. "I'd love to fuck it."

I smiled. "I bet you would."

I spread my legs as wide as I could. I leaned back, using one hand against his leg to brace myself. The other hand I moved slowly between my legs. I watched his eyes begin to glow as I worked first one finger and then two inside my tight wet hole.

"It's bigger than two fingers," he teased.

"Got to start somewhere," I gasped.

I moved slowly up his body letting my breasts rub over his cock on my way. When I reached his chest I stood. His breath quickened when I unlaced my tunic and slipped out one breast.

"Can I not see both?" he asked.

"Not until you show me all of you," I said. "Until you show me your naked body as a man, this tunic remains on."

He licked his lips. "That's fair."

I leaned forward, pressing one breast into his face. "Suck my nipple."

Without hesitation he worked his long tongue around the already taut peak and I cried out. I threw my head back as he pulled more of my flesh into his mouth.

He pulled back suddenly. "I could get you ready with my hands if you'd let me."

"The chain stays where it is, Wolf."

I braced myself against the tree and used what remained of a broken branch to lift myself. I put one booted foot on each side of his head as I crouched low over his face. "Lick it," I commanded, thrusting my pussy toward his mouth.

It was all I could do to maintain my grip on the branch as he licked my slit from top to bottom. Finally, when my entire body shook with both the effort to hold myself up and to keep from coming, I pushed away from the tree and released the branch.

I landed with one foot squarely on either side of his hips. His fully erect cock rose to meet me.

I crouched over him and rubbed the tip of his cock back and forth over my wet sex, using my juices to coat his length.

"I wonder if this is considered poaching," I mused.

He gasped as I stroked him again, then laughed. "How did you arrive at such a question?"

"Well, here I am taking this wild cock for myself without anyone's permission. Is fucking a werewolf in the Comte's woods a crime?"

"I'm sure he won't mind."

"I wouldn't be so certain."

I kept my eyes focused on his face as I began to lower myself onto him.

"Oh," he gasped.

I kept one hand between us, using it to stroke my pussy lips, guiding myself farther down. I took as much of him as I could before moving back up, stroking him as I did so, then guiding myself back down. I moaned as my sex stretched tight. It was a wonderful sensation somewhere between pain and pleasure.

I leaned forward to brace myself on his chest and as I did so I accidentally pressed the chain harder against his skin. I paused at his sharp intake of breath, realizing what I'd done.

"I'm sorry," I said, breathlessly.

"Press it against my nipple," he growled. When I hesitated he said, "Do it while you ride me."

His eyes glowed brighter in the growing darkness as the sun set behind us. The silver sizzled as I pressed it hard against his skin and rode his enormous cock as hard and fast as I could.

"Yeeesssss," he growled. "Fuck me harder."

"You're burning," I gasped. I could feel the warmth beneath my hand as smoke rose from his flesh.

His voice deepened as he repeated, "Fuck. Me. Harder."

The combination of sex and violence aroused me in a way I'd never experienced before. I came so hard and so suddenly that all I could do was cling to his shoulders and scream.

He lifted his hips, thrusting into me as I held him, his breathing coming faster and faster.

"Yes, hold onto me while I fill your pussy up," he growled.

His howl echoed through the woods as he pumped his hot seed into me. I felt it pour out of me with a rush of heat, spilling onto us both. As his cock began to shrink in size, I was at last able to sit down on him completely.

When I realized the chain was still burning him I quickly leaned to the side and released the loose knot. I removed the silver from his chest and without stopping to think, pressed a kiss to the burn mark.

"It will heal quickly," he said, wrapping his arms around me.

In that moment I knew that not only had he allowed the silver chain for my benefit, he had me now, and it was *I* who was at *his* mercy.

"Relax, little red," he said softly. "Let me hold you."

Chapter Sixteen

Belladonna

When I woke up, resting against his big chest, I couldn't believe I'd fallen asleep like this. It was not fear or even cold that had awakened me, but the soft press of a kiss against the top of my head. Even though he had the lips of a wolf, the feel of a kiss is unmistakable.

I sat up, realizing that I had been resting against his enormous body like a piece of furniture. He had pulled my red cloak over us. Between the cloak and the warmth of his body, I was more comfortable than I wanted to admit. For a moment all I wanted to do was curl up against his warmth and forget the rest of the world even existed.

"What is it?" he asked.

"I wasn't expecting this."

"Are you upset because I kissed you?"

I shook my head. "It is the tenderness of your touch that surprises me."

He cupped my face gently with one clawed hand. "Am I not allowed some tenderness?"

"I just wasn't expecting it, that's all," I said softly. "There is something I should tell you."

He sat up then, but still held me in his arms, wrapped in my red cloak.

"That is never a good thing to hear, especially not after an encounter like we just had."

"The Comte's late father and my grandmother were friends. Both families are originally from the village of Gévaudan, and as I understand it, they hunted together."

"They hunted *werewolves* together?"

I nodded. "The Comte and I are the last of two long lines of werewolf hunters. His father and my grandmother decided that if I was not married or betrothed by my twenty fifth birthday, and if he also remained unattached, I would marry Maroc d'Ulfric."

"He is older than you, correct?" he asked.

"He is, ten years. And my twenty fifth birthday was last month. He has sent invitations that I have politely declined since then. But a deal is a deal, and I can't refuse him any longer. We're to formalize our engagement in a few days' time. I'm sure the wedding will follow soon after."

For a few moments there was nothing but the sounds of the night echoing around us. The cries of owls and insects seemed magnified as I awaited his response.

"What do you think of him?" he said at last.

"The Comte? I don't actually know him. I've never even seen him. My grandmother swears I saw him once when I was a child, but I have no memory of this."

Even in the faint moonlight streaming through the canopy of trees I could see his surprise.

"Really? In all the times you've visited your friend at the castle, you've never seen him?"

"I've heard he's a giant, nearly seven feet tall, but handsome. I believe my friend who works at the castle used the word 'formidable.'"

"And you've *never* seen him, not even once?"

"Not even once."

"Does this bother you?" he asked.

"Not really. I've no interest in anyone else and being so big … maybe he'll have a nice size cock." I meant this as a joke and actually expected Wolf to laugh.

I was surprised when a big hand smacked me on the arse. "No interest in anyone else, eh?"

"We've only just met, you and I." I put my hand on his chest and with a heavy sigh, forced myself to get up from his lap. "This agreement was made years ago and I will at least give the man a chance."

His hand wrapped possessively around one of my thighs before releasing me with a growl. As I cleaned myself up and got dressed he watched me. Several times he looked like he wanted to say something, but all he ended up saying was, "Good night, little red," as I turned to leave.

Chapter Seventeen

Wolf/Maroc

I kept my distance, but followed her home. I wanted to be certain she was safe before I returned to the castle. I watched her enter the safety of her home, and waited until I saw a lantern light up in an upstairs window. Her bedroom. She was just about to lift the tunic over her head when she smiled and closed the curtains. Did she know I was out there?

She told me about her grandmother's spells of protection. Surely she knows that if I meant her any harm at all I would not be able to get this close. Perhaps that is why she finally removed the silver chain. The way she looked at me tonight, the way she smiled ... the feel of her sleeping on me, breathing softly against my chest. It did things to my heart I had not anticipated.

I ran back through the woods with one reoccurring thought, *"What mess have I gotten myself into?"*

I'm to be married to, and meet in my human form very soon, a woman who enjoys fucking a werewolf. Is that a good thing for me or not?

How should I begin to tell her what I am? I feel like I need to reassure her again that I am not the killer on the loose in the countryside. After all, she has heard rumors of a powerful alpha male and I fit that description better than most. That scent I caught a hint of though ... I can only pray it is *not* the wolf I think it is. That wolf should be long dead. Then I remembered something, the she-wolf I'd killed referred to someone named Gaston. I'd been so caught up in the fight and then making sure Bella was safe, that her words didn't truly resonate until this moment.

"Oh, damn," I gasped. "It must be him."

The wolf who murdered my father and made me the monster I am today, his name was Gaston.

Then again, Gaston is one of the most common names in all of France, I reminded myself. There was still the slightest chance I could be mistaken. After all, she never said the Gaston she was talking about was also a werewolf. She did hint at it though, didn't she?

"A werewolf can't regrow a head, can it?" I asked, continuing to talk to myself as I trotted through the woods. I had *never* heard of a werewolf surviving being decapitated and I cut his head off myself with my silver sword. I saw his head fall back, hanging by a thread as his body hit the ground.

"It could be someone survived from his former pack, someone who knows how terrifying he was. Now they are using that name to scare the hell out of people, like me."

Despite the threat that remained, like a man possessed, my thoughts kept returning to Bella.

It was not my intention to meet her that first day, but I did, and I did so as a beast. I had to find a way to tell her who I really am without looking as though I'd been toying with her.

"What if when we meet she doesn't like the way I look as a man?" I worried.

I stopped running and took a deep breath. "One thing at a time," I said out loud to myself. "After we officially meet, if we still get along well, I will find a way to tell her. After all we have shared, I believe she will be open to the idea."

"But what if she prefers me as Wolf?" my mind asked, like a little devil on my shoulder. *"She thinks you are two separate men."*

"Sometimes I wonder if I am," I said out loud.

It was in this moment I realized I'd stopped running in the middle of the road. A man leading a donkey from the direction of Pomme de Terre had stopped in his tracks and was staring at me with a mixture of fascination and horror.

The situation would have been awkward even if I looked like a man. But it was made ridiculous by the fact that he'd just walked up on a werewolf talking to himself in the middle of the road.

He reeked of alcohol and I assumed he was on his way back from The Salted Pork. I opened my arms wide and laughed.

"Women! Who understands their motivations, am I right?"

The man screamed, leapt onto the donkey and rode in the opposite direction, still yelling like a banshee.

Chapter Eighteen

Gaston

"Please, stop!" the man yelled.

I yawned and reclined back into my temporary throne. It was the last remnant of my former glory. An oversized gilded chair with red velvet cushions. It was fitted with poles so that my subordinates could carry me, if I wished. And it was large enough to accommodate both of my forms.

"Do you have any idea how many times I've heard those words?"

"Or some variation thereof," the witch said, smiling back at me.

She raised her knife again and the bound man began to cry.

"Tell us what we want to know and you are free," I said casually. "Why does everyone find that so difficult?"

"Maybe it's the spell," Jules, my beta wolf suggested.

I glared at him. "A spell cannot be responsible for *everything*."

"Oh, but it can," the witch said. "You underestimate her power."

I rose slowly and walked over to where she stood. There were three men chained to the wall in the crumbling castle where we'd decided to camp. For the time being, the place was perfect. There was space to torture and enough rooms for everyone to sleep and have some degree of privacy. But this room, like many others, had a ceiling that was open to the stars. The cannon ball that opened it up decades ago still rested in the far corner beside a large brazier.

"The woman whose body you were found standing over, her name was Minerva," I said to him.

Even though neither of us made a move to strike him again he trembled.

"She meant a great deal to me. You see, several years ago she saved my life, when many would have left me to die." I opened the collar of my shirt and revealed the thin red line that ran all the way around my neck. "She sewed my head back onto my body and used any means necessary to keep me alive. I think it only left a scar because of the silver sword, but it continues to fade."

"Please," he begged, crying hysterically.

"Shut up," I growled. "I'm trying to tell you a story." I straightened my shirt and continued. "As I was saying, she saved me. Hunters left me for dead, and I would have been if not for her.

She was the only surviving member of my pack and my neck was only attached by the barest shred of flesh. Even *I* didn't know I could survive such an injury."

"If I knew what you wanted, *monsieur*, I would give it to you," the man beside him whimpered.

"I believe they hold their tongues due to her spell," the witch said. "Perhaps their lack of answers is not their fault. Even you cannot yet recall her name."

If she wasn't so beautiful, I would have hit her for that. "Not yet," I growled. I turned my attention back to the men on the wall. "What happened in that clearing?"

"I don't know," the first man said. "We were looking for a place to make camp and when we came into the clearing ... we just found her there."

"Not only was her heart missing, someone pissed on her corpse," I said, snapping my teeth in his direction.

"It wasn't us!" he yelled. "We didn't even touch her!"

"It's true," the second man said. "We had barely found her before you found us. We only knew there was a dead, naked woman in a clearing. That's it."

"That's it?" I shrugged. "Well, someone pissed on her, but I think we can all agree it wasn't any of you. That was werewolf urine."

At the mention of werewolves they both began to tremble again. The third man remained oddly silent.

"Who or what, precisely, are you looking for?" the second man asked.

I found I could not directly answer him. Instead, I continued my story.

"It took me years to realize I was being misled by magic. And it took me even more years to find a witch powerful enough to get me this close to her. Then I had to recover from being decapitated." I looked from one man to the other. "The huntress who killed my brother. Her name seems always on the tip of my tongue, just beyond my reach. She is a legend. I hear people speak her name and yet I cannot comprehend or recall their words. Neither can anyone intent on harming her or her family." I sighed. "What a clever old cunt."

"A huntress?" the first man asked. "You mean to say that a *woman* has thwarted your every move?"

I growled. "Careful how you word your responses with me. Have you seen them? I know there are two of them now. They wear red cloaks." Even saying this much caused me physical pain. It felt as if someone was strangling me, trying to keep the words from leaving my mouth.

At the mention of the red cloaks the eyes of the third man widened. He knew something. Maybe he really couldn't speak due to a spell.

"I don't know anything," the first man said.

"Then you are of no use to me."

In an instant claws extended from the fingertips of my right hand. The men watched, wide-eyed while my arm transformed from the elbow down. I laughed as they screamed.

I looked down at the witch. By the way my eyes burned I knew they had changed as well.

"Didn't you say that you needed human entrails for your next spell?" I asked her.

"And a heart," she said, smiling. "Minerva was supposed to have brought me the ingredients."

The first man's tunic was already torn open. I sank my claws slowly into the flesh just below his ribs, savoring the sounds he made and the feeling of his flesh giving way beneath my touch.

"Please!" the second man screamed. "Have mercy!"

"What a wonderful idea," I agreed. With these words I ripped downward, spilling the first man's guts onto the stone floor. "I have not had Mercy all day. Not a single drop."

The witch laughed as I bowed to the men and gestured toward her. "Gentlemen, meet, Mercy, the woman who is helping me to achieve my revenge."

Without another word I grabbed her by the throat with my monstrous hand. She laughed as the man's blood was smeared across her bronze skin. I lifted her onto the nearby table and without a care as to who watched us, I lifted her skirts. The claws of my other hand grew and I used them to shred her pantalettes.

"I liked those," she gasped.

"You like this cock," I growled. I used my claws to tear open the front of my trousers as her sultry laughter filled the room once more.

I shoved her thighs wider apart and without further preamble, thrust into her deeply.

She screamed, but a wicked smile curved her lips.

"He said I should have Mercy," I growled. I leaned down as if to kiss her, but stopped short of contact, snapping my teeth at her lips. "Should we give them the full performance?"

"Fuck them," she said, reaching around to grab my ass. "Give it to *me*."

"Oh? Do you think you've earned it?" As we spoke I continued to thrust into her, hard and unrelenting. "You have yet to completely break her spell. I still can't remember her name. They obviously know who I'm referring to and they can't even describe her to me!"

The angrier I became the harder I throttled her cunt.

"Fuck me like the monster I know you are or I might decide to stop helping you," she taunted.

"You drive a hard bargain," I growled.

I let the beast take me as I looked down at her. Where I had seen this twist the features of so many with fear, hers were transformed with delight.

My feet tore through my boots, as my thighs ripped through my trousers. Mercy reached up to stroke my long wolf face as I pumped in and out of her. The sounds of me striking against her wet flesh echoed off the stone walls.

I didn't realize the first man was still alive until I heard him mewling pitifully at the sight of us.

I began to grow inside of her and felt her muscles contract around me, tightening with her release.

~ 155 ~

"After I finally kill her, I'm going after Maroc," I groaned, still fucking her hard. "I'll give him the honor of being the last werewolf hunter in the region before I take his head."

"Why?" she panted.

"Because he is the only one to get close enough to cut off my head. He must have at least suspected by now that I've returned, that he didn't finish the job he and his father were hired for. I'm sure his fear grows with every death."

With that thought I exploded inside of her, my hot release gushing from her wide open cunt and pouring onto the table.

"Get to work on those spells," I said, pulling my cock out of her.

I walked over to the first man and found him still breathing, but only barely. "Well, aren't you the survivor." I thrust my hand into his chest and pulled out his heart. The other men screamed as I tossed it onto the table beside Mercy. "I believe you said you needed this."

I turned back to the still screaming men. "The two of you better start thinking very hard about what you can tell me about a huntress who wears a red cloak."

Chapter Nineteen

Belladonna

Maroc d'Ulfric sent an answer to my message the very next day. I woke early to find a deer, fully cleaned and dressed, in a sack on our front porch. This message was clearly an apology from Wolf, for interrupting my hunt. I smiled with the memory of everything that happened afterwards.

My grandmother was hanging part of the venison in our smokehouse when a messenger arrived. The Comte asked for a week to prepare for a celebration.

Tonight half the village will be in the castle's courtyard to celebrate our engagement.

"I never thought *I* would say this, but you should probably wear a dress," my grandmother said to me.

Cherry had been given permission from the Comte to leave her duties at the castle and come visit me today.

"How did he know we are friends?" I asked her.

She shrugged. "He must have seen us together at some point. Doesn't the entire village know we are like sisters?"

"More like the two of you terrorized everyone when you were children," my grandmother joked.

He probably thought Cherry would help me prepare for the occasion, but I honestly didn't need any help.

"Perhaps you could compromise," Cherry suggested. "You don't have to dress entirely like a man, at the very least."

I laughed. "I do *not* look anything like a man, regardless of how I choose to dress."

"You're about to be a comtesse," my grandmother said. "At least try to look more …"

"More what?"

"Appropriate for the occasion," Cherry said, smiling.

"My grandmother is going to pour a potion into the wine tonight known as a 'blessing.' If I wore nothing but a strip of cloth to cover my womanly bits and danced around a fire, I'd still be appropriately dressed for a blessing from the old gods."

"A what?" Cherry asked, looking alarmed. "Are we all supposed to drink this?"

My grandmother's husky laughter echoed in the warmth of my bedroom where the three of us were gathered.

"Don't frighten her, child," she said. "And yes, I hope that everyone at the gathering tonight will partake."

"May I ask what is in this *blessing*?"

Firelight and mischief reflected in her eyes as my grandmother replied, "Magic."

"And some small white mushrooms from the forest," I added.

Cherry looked even more concerned when my grandmother and I both laughed.

"You've had them before," I told her.

"Yes, and I thought I was a rabbit for *three days*. I was hopping through the bloody forest in a blue bonnet that I fully believed hid my long ears from everyone else."

My grandmother laughed until her eyes filled with tears. "You will have the time of your life," she said at last. "But if you'd prefer to *not* become a rabbit for three days, I suggest you limit your wine consumption this evening."

I was staring into the wardrobe at the few dresses I owned. "I have an idea."

*****

When the Comte's carriage arrived for us I was wearing tight black leggings made of soft woven cloth this time rather than leather. My knee-high boots were polished more than I

~ 159 ~

think they'd been in the entire time I'd owned
them. I took the long ruffled sash from my red
silk dress and tied it around my waist. It was
meant to drape down the back of a matching
skirt, but I wore it so the front was open
revealing my leggings and the ruffles fell down
the backs of my legs. The matching coat was
short with a high collar. It fit me in a way that
revealed my every curve. The ensemble was
completed with black lace gloves that I'd long
since cut the fingers out of.

My grandmother had pulled back my long
hair in a swirl of braids that were stacked high
at the crown and fell in loose waves down my
back. My hair was held in place by pins and
decorated by dozens of tiny white flowers. The
cosmetics I'd decided on looked very much like
what my grandmother and I wore on a hunt. I
did this because having to face everyone as the
future comtesse felt a bit like walking into a
battle. No one outside of our two families knew
of the agreement between us. So, naturally
gossip had been spreading throughout the
region like wildfire for the past week.

Cherry told me that as soon as Maroc
announced our engagement and began to make
preparations people started asking if I was
pregnant. A few even asked her if marriage to

the Comte was part of my reward for our recent werewolf hunt.

Before we went out to the carriage I asked them, "How do I look?"

"Bold," Cherry said. "And beautiful, like some wild and untamable goddess."

Islene gave her a look and raised one brow. "Have you already been into the mushrooms while I got dressed?"

My grandmother was wearing a high-waisted dress made of black muslin and embroidered with golden leaves. Her hair and cosmetics looked much like mine.

Cherry was wearing a similarly styled frock of blue silk with a pale green shawl. Both colors complimented her long blond hair that she'd left unbound.

"You look beautiful," my grandmother said, turning her attention back to me. "Now, shall we get this evening started?"

It was nearly an hour on horseback from our home to the castle. That is, if you have a fast horse. Either way the time seemed to fly by. We passed so many people from the village, all going in the same direction, dressed in their best clothes.

"Everyone is staring at me," I said, leaning back from the window. "Even more than usual."

"Then smile and wave," my grandmother said, her voice full of sarcasm. "Give the bastards something to talk about."

"After everyone drinks that wine tonight, I think they'll have plenty to talk about," Cherry said.

"Oh, yes. For quite some time," my grandmother agreed.

As the carriage made its way up the long winding drive to the castle I could see someone standing near the open gates.

"That's the Comte," Cherry gasped. "He came out to greet you himself."

"Is that wrong?" I asked.

"It isn't correct etiquette. You should be brought to him and properly introduced."

Says the woman who can't stop screwing the cook on the table where part of tonight's meal was likely prepared, I thought. I bit my lip to keep from saying this out loud.

"Your knowledge of etiquette certainly outweighs mine," I said instead.

I shrugged and leaned toward the window again to get a better look at him.

"Don't stare," Cherry said, laughing.

My grandmother laughed then too. "Nothing wrong with admiring the view."

"I am *very* happy to see he doesn't adhere to the current fashions for nobility," I said. I only knew of such things from a few nobles we'd met in years past through hunting jobs, and from what Cherry told me of visitors to the castle. "Those short breeches and stockings make a man look more like he'd enjoy receiving a cock rather than give one."

My grandmother snorted with laughter as Cherry said, "Do *not* say that the first time you meet him, please."

"She isn't wrong though," grandmother said. "Those awful breeches make their balls gather oddly to one side, leaving their cocks confused as to where they should fit."

Cherry was laughing as she said, "He dresses as he likes, regardless of fashion. However, we are *not* going to sit around a table for your *engagement* and discuss cocks and balls with the Comte."

"Why not? He should know what he's getting, don't you think?" I asked.

About that time I realized how much closer we were and I got a much better look at my betrothed.

His beauty was devastating. I'd never seen a man like him, and he was *tall*. Nearly as tall as my Wolf.

My Wolf? Where had that thought come from?

The Comte was positively magnificent. He turned to speak to a man as he approached, giving a view of his long dark hair pulled back tightly and secured at the nape of his neck. He was dressed entirely in black. The full-length trousers he wore were tight, very tight, and revealed every muscular curve of his legs as he walked slowly toward the carriage. He moved with the fluid grace of a dancer, or an animal of prey.

His coat was open and was shorter in front, but not as short as the current trend. Instead it reached to the tops of his well-sculpted thighs, leaving the back to fall to his knees. The coat was embroidered with silver thread. The matching vest accentuated his broad chest and narrow waist as he moved. The tunic he wore beneath was black and rather than wear a cravat it was left open, revealing what I'm sure would be considered by others to be a scandalous amount of flesh. I, on the other hand, found this look to be very arousing. In fact, everything about the Comte was very much to my liking.

When the carriage stopped he reached us in two long strides and without hesitation opened the door.

"I'm so pleased you've come," he said smoothly.

Though he addressed us all, his gaze immediately found mine. His eyes were the color of honeyed tea and his smile reached them easily.

"Belladonna LaCroix, what made you finally accept my invitations?"

His voice was rich and warm, like a fine liquor. The sound made me instantly wet. He could have read the dullest book aloud to me and I would sit and listen, panting with desire.

My first thought was, *"Well, most recently I've started fucking a werewolf."* But of course, I did not say that.

"Can I have a glass of wine at least, before I answer that question?" I said, accepting the hand he offered me.

His smile made my heart flutter and my pussy clench.

"As you like," he said.

The other man I'd seen him talking to helped Cherry and my grandmother from the carriage as I hooked my arm through his and let Maroc lead me into the castle.

I had been to the castle many times, but never gone beyond the kitchen and some of the servants quarters in back. I had never seen the front entrance up close, let alone been led through the front hall. I didn't want to look like a pauper in the presence of wealth for the first time, but I couldn't seem to stop myself from staring.

"Do you like the decorations?" he asked, looking down at me. "Islene told me you like roses. I've had as many clipped from the gardens as possible without leaving the bushes bare."

I laughed softly. "It's lovely."

"Lovely" didn't do justice to the grandeur of the decorations, nor to the castle itself. I'd never imagined the parts I hadn't seen could be so impressive. Which immediately brought my mind back to the Comte and those tight trousers.

"It's a pleasure to finally meet you, after knowing for years now that we were supposed to be married," he said.

"You might want to get to know me before you decide if that's a pleasure or not."

His laughter was soft, yet knowing and masculine. I immediately loved the sound.

"The agreement between my grandmother and your father said that we should marry if you and were both still unattached by the time I turned twenty five. Why did you choose to wait until then to reach out to me?" I asked.

"I wanted to give you every possible opportunity to find someone you desired, without pushing my presence into your life in any way."

"You were giving me time to meet someone else?"

He looked down at me again and smiled broadly. "You know, a decent man."

I laughed, louder this time. "Comte d'Ulfric, are you telling me you are indecent?"

He stopped walking and turned slightly to face me. "Can you honestly say you'd waste your time with a man who isn't? And please, call me Maroc."

With a wink he took my arm once more and we resumed our walk through the front of the castle toward the courtyard.

Two well-dressed men opened a set of doors in front of us and I tried not to look overly impressed as I let the Comte lead me through.

The courtyard was massive. The castle circled the grounds, leaving an enormous space that was already filled with lavishly decorated tables and chairs. In the middle of the gathered tables was an enormous bonfire, waiting to be lit.

To our right was a small band of musicians tuning their instruments. Servants were bringing out dishes of food and placing them just so onto every surface available.

"If this is our engagement celebration, what did you have in mind for the wedding?" I asked, half joking.

"Is it too much?" he asked. "I wanted you to know how happy I was that this was finally happening, but I didn't mean to take things too far."

I smiled up at him, unable to help myself. "I love it. I think tonight will be … interesting."

"Oh, I hope I can do better than that."

He led me to the farthest table. It was long and heavily decorated, and it faced both the bonfire and the emerging crowd of guests.

"How many people are coming?" I asked.

He pulled out a chair directly in the middle of the table that resembled a throne with black velvet cushions. He indicated that I should sit, so I did, still waiting for an answer.

"As many as the courtyard can hold," he said, smiling. "I want the village to feel that they are a part of this."

He must have noticed my unease.

"I should have asked if such a crowd was all right with you," he said softly. "I'm sorry."

I shook my head as he sat down beside me. "It isn't that. I've always had the impression that a lot of the villagers don't like me because …" I searched for the right words.

Maroc reached over and gently took my hand. "You are different," he said simply. "People fear what they do not understand. You are also beautiful and I imagine that more than a few of them are very jealous."

I squeezed his big warm hand in return. "Do you always know the right thing to say?"

He smiled again. "Oh, not at all. Just wait, I'm overdue for a stupid remark. Any minute now."

He looked at me then and took both of my hands. "Bella, may I call you that?"

I nodded.

"I want you to know that you are not obligated to me in any way. Even after tonight, if this is something you don't want to do, then say so. I realize it will take some time for us to truly get to know one another. But if you have no interest in being with me, in upholding an agreement to a stranger, I understand. I am happy you are here, but you don't owe me anything."

In that instant I knew that I really liked Maroc.

Chapter Twenty

Belladonna

I lost track of my grandmother and Cherry in the crowd until I saw them approaching our table.

My grandmother smiled at Maroc as if they shared a joke. He rose and gave her a short bow. "Islene, so glad you are here."

"Could I have a word?" she asked. "Before the wine is served, preferably."

He gave her an easy smile. "Of course." He turned to me and said, "Please, excuse me while I finish some last minute preparations for our party."

I gave my grandmother a questioning look, but didn't say anything as she and Maroc walked through a door on the left side of the courtyard. I wondered if he had any idea how devious she could be or what she had planned. I also wondered *how* she was going to get away with it.

"Lost in thought?" Cherry sat down on my other side and the sound of her voice made me jump with surprise.

"Sorry," she said, laughing. "I'm assuming Islene is off to *bless* the wine for tonight's gathering."

I laughed then too. "Most likely."

"She only brought one small bottle. How is that going to be enough?"

"Magic. If my understanding of this particular concoction is correct, even a single drop goes a long way. She also has a pouch of finely chopped dried mushrooms hidden underneath her dress."

"Of course she does," Cherry said, shaking her head. "So, what do you think about Maroc d'Ulfric?"

"It's too soon to form a real opinion."

"You know that's not what I meant."

"He's easily the most lust-worthy man I've ever seen."

She laughed. "I told you so. He's always been kind to everyone on staff. I've worked here for five years now and never seen him talk down to anyone or be stern for no reason. I believe that once you get to know each other, you'll be a good match." She paused for a moment before asking in a hushed tone, "What about your werewolf?"

"What do you mean?"

Additional goblets were being placed on the tables as most of the guests had arrived. We stopped talking when someone approached our table with a large pie. I smiled when I saw it was the cook, Armand, and the way he was looking at Cherry.

"Are you enjoying your time off, my lady," he drawled mockingly.

"It's only for today," she said. "Besides, it's not as if you aren't being well compensated to work during the celebration. I saw the casks of wine the Comte had set aside, specifically for the staff working tonight. *We* will all be drunk tonight and tomorrow will be *your* day off. No one will need the services of a maid until afterwards anyway."

He winked at her. "By the way, I expect a show of gratitude once this is all over."

She laughed. "Is the pie going to be that good?"

"I'm the one who told him Bella is your closest friend and suggested you might be able to make this night a better experience for her if you could share it together."

I smiled then. "So, it was you."

He gave me a slight nod. "He was talking to me about what dishes he wanted to be served and asked about a rumor that you had a good friend who worked here."

Cherry and Armand flirted shamelessly for another moment while I turned my attention back to the sight of Maroc walking across the length of the courtyard. His long strides were purposeful and when he saw me watching him, he never took his eyes off mine.

"Well, what do you plan to do about your werewolf?" Cherry asked again.

I broke eye contact with the Comte then to give my friend a surprised look. I realized a moment later that Armand had gone and no one else seemed to be listening to us.

"Did you think I would ask such a thing in front of Armand?" she laughed. "I would like an answer though. It's quite the interesting situation you've gotten yourself into."

I gave her a wry grin. "You're enjoying this."

"Every moment. It's better than a good book. I can't wait to see what happens next."

As Maroc got closer I lowered my voice and replied, "If I had an answer, I would give it to you."

Cherry gasped and put a hand over her breasts in mock surprise. "You have *feelings* for this werewolf."

"Shhhh."

"Oh, this *is* getting interesting," she said. "In a perfect world, you could have them both, eh?"

"By the balls of the old gods, Cherry, now that image is in my mind." I couldn't help but laugh.

"You're welcome," she quipped.

Maroc reached us about that time and when I turned slightly toward him I found myself directly facing his cock. I paused for too long, staring at the large bulge in his tight black trousers before looking up at his face.

His smile could not have been any more wicked. "Shall we get this celebration started?" he asked me.

He definitely caught me staring at his crotch. Though I am not easily embarrassed I could feel my face burning. The first time I meet the man and I get caught admiring his package as if I expected it to greet me somehow.

Maroc waved toward the performers and the music quickly ceased.

"If you could give me your attention please," he called.

A man behind him rang a symbol, and those who were not close enough to hear his voice, or were talking too loudly, quickly silenced themselves.

"Friends and neighbors, we are here tonight to celebrate the soon-to-be joining of two once great families of werewolf hunters." He laughed. "I'm sorry, that sounded a bit bleak for an introduction."

A few laughs echoed throughout the crowd.

I noticed then that servers were walking among those gathered, making sure everyone's goblets were filled with wine.

"Belladonna LaCroix, of the famed LaCroix hunters, has graciously agreed to be my bride."

He paused for applause and cheers as he turned to me with a smile.

"If there is one thing that hunting werewolves taught me, it's that you do not always have the time you think you have. Bearing that in mind, if it is all right with you, Bella, I would like for everyone to meet us here again, two weeks from now, for our wedding ceremony."

Cheers rang out from the crowd and I felt like my heart stopped. It was obvious that Maroc was awaiting my response. I opened my mouth, but no sound came out. I knew he wanted to get married soon, but *two weeks*? I had thought at least a month.

His smile began to slip around the edges. I couldn't leave him hanging like this.

"Yes," I said softly. It was all I could manage to say.

His smile returned and he faced the crowd once more. "Raise your cups with me tonight friends. Let's eat, let's drink, and someone light this bonfire!"

"Woooooooo!!!!" The crowd roared.

He lifted his goblet and rank deeply. Well, *merde*. I wanted to warn him about the wine first.

Maroc sat back down beside me and the noise of the party resumed along with the music.

"You didn't seem happy about that time frame at all," he said softly. "Would you like the ceremony delayed further? I should have asked you this in private." He laughed nervously. "See, I told you I was overdue to say something stupid. When your response before said for me to take charge of the planning .... well, I took charge of the planning. If I'm being honest, I was afraid that your response showed a lack of interest."

He moved as if to run a hand through his long hair, then remembered it was tied back and stopped himself.

"Just know that even right up until we take our vows, you can always walk away from me and I will understand." He winked then and reached for his wine. "If you wait until after the vows, at least bed me before you disappear."

He was just about to take a drink when I slapped my hand over the goblet. He raised a brow and I couldn't believe he looked even more charming.

"Do you know what is in this wine?" I asked softly, trying to be sure no one else heard me.

His smile was devilish as he slowly removed my hand, maintaining eye contact as he took a sip. He sat the wine aside as he replied, "Who do you think I let Islene into the storeroom?"

My startled expression made him laugh.

"So, my grandmother asked to pour a hallucinogen into the wine and you simply agreed?"

"Bella, I know what you and your grandmother are, just as my father knew. This is also not the first time I've had these mushrooms."

"I have to say, you are nothing at all like what I expected," I said.

He reached for my wine and passed it to me. As I accepted the goblet my fingers brushed over his. Even this slight contact sent a spark through me.

"And what did you expect?" he asked. "Some pompous cunt with a stick up his arse?"

My laughter was sudden and loud, causing a few people to stare. Fuck them. I was actually beginning to enjoy myself.

"I expected ..."

As I tried to find the right words he reached out and tucked a stray hair behind my ear. Oh, yes. I wanted this man. Badly. Everything about him aroused a desire in me the likes of which I'd only felt for Wolf. Damn, Wolf. What was I going to say to him? He knew about this, about tonight. But now everything was so much more *real*. Maroc deserved someone who would be faithful. I already liked him enough to not want to cause him any pain.

"Where did you go just now?" Maroc asked softly. "Because your thoughts were clearly not here."

"I didn't expect to find someone I could relate to," I said at last.

He tapped the side of my goblet. "Then let's take this journey together tonight. Let the old gods give us their blessing and see where that takes us."

I turned up my goblet and for some fool reason, I drank every last drop.

Chapter Twenty One

Maroc

I could feel the mushrooms beginning to take effect. My body felt lighter and my heart raced. And beside me was the most beautiful woman in the world. The way her red hair seemed to capture the light of all the torches and the bonfire, it put me into a kind of trance. I knew in that moment that I was falling in love with her.

That first day in the forest, I only wanted to get a look at the woman I was supposed to soon marry. Everything that happened afterwards was more than I could have hoped for. And now, here she was. So much death around us and here was the breath of life, this vibrant flame of a woman sitting next to me.

"Why don't I tell her tonight?" I thought. *"Tell her that I am Wolf and let everything be out in the open between us."*

After all, that was why she hesitated in her response before, wasn't it? She feels something for me, only she does not know it is *me* she cares for.

I realized I'd been staring at her when Bella smiled at me and asked, "Does this bother you?"

She gestured to her body. It took me a moment to understand her meaning.

"The outfit, you mean?"

She nodded. Her cheeks were flushed as if from arousal, but I knew it was a combination of wine and other intoxicants.

"Most of the time, I wear leather. I was recently informed by the baker's wife that she could see the imprint of my sex through my leggings. Apparently, that is not appropriate for a decent woman, let alone a comtesse."

Her bluntness and vulgarity were making me hard. I tried to hide this with my coat.

"Are you asking if, once we are married, will I mind you wearing the leathers of a hunter? Or are you asking if I care what the baker's wife thinks?"

Her smile made my heart feel lighter somehow.

"Either," she said.

I leaned closer to her as I said, "I don't care if you stuff them halfway up your pretty little pussy. But what do I know about fashion?" I winked and took another sip of wine. "I'm no baker's wife."

Her laughter was rough and sensual. "Is it all right if I tell you how much I enjoy hearing you say the word *pussy*," she purred softly.

"Two weeks from now we will be married and you can do much more than hear me say it," I replied.

Much to my delight she flushed deeper. Knowing her as I already did, I'd say that was a flush of arousal this time and certainly not embarrassment.

"I didn't expect to like you so much," she said suddenly.

"My God, you really were expecting some boring wretch."

She laughed again and I saw tears glistening in her warm brown eyes. "I really was," she confessed.

A yell went up from the crowd and I realized that everyone else was feeling the effects of the wine as well, some much more than others.

"Who is the shirtless man that just started dancing around the fire?" she asked, looking amused.

"That's Hans, one of the stable hands." I laughed as Hans began to pull random people from the crowd to join him.

"He's got some nice dance moves," she quipped, raising one curved brow.

I rose slowly and let my coat fall back into my chair. "You only think so because you've never seen me dance."

"You? Dance like this?" She laughed. "This is not some memorized pattern of steps for a grand ball, *Comte*. The way that man is dancing is *wild*. Every thrust of his hips is a cry to Mother Nature and to the spirits that dwell in these old woods. He may not even know it, but he is praying with his body. He is asking for the blessing of the gods."

I smiled as I held out my hand to her. "It is our union they're celebrating. Should we not ask along with him?"

As we made our way closer to the fire it seemed as if the entire courtyard had broken out in fits of dancing. The music had taken on a more primal rhythm and as Bella looked at me she tore open the front of her coat. Her tunic hung open partially, revealing the creamy curves of the tops of her breasts.

With a sultry grin she took my hand and placed it directly over her heart.

"*This* is the dance," she said breathlessly. "*This* is the only rhythm you need to follow."

Normally, her actions would have sent cries of shock throughout the gathered crowd. But when I glanced around I saw that much more shocking actions were going on all around us.

"This is more .... *bawdy* than I expected," I confessed.

She smiled as she moved closer to me, all the while holding my hand to her breast.

"Are you shaken? Does the display of these villagers offend your delicate sensibilities?" she teased.

"Me? Delicate?" When I threw back my head to laugh my hair came unbound. The look of pure hunger in her eyes let me know that Bella preferred it that way.

I smiled down at her and my heart began to beat in time to the drums of the musicians. "I'm afraid our height difference might make dancing difficult," I said.

The crowd of dancers, at least thirty now around the fire, continued to twirl and undulate around us.

"Then I will climb you like a tree if necessary," she said.

With those words she began to move and I followed. The drums beat faster as the courtyard swirled around us. I followed the trail of her flaming hair through the crowd.

Round and round the fire we danced. She grabbed my hand, pulling our bodies together in an embrace. Her hair had come completely unbound and wild curls spilled over her shoulders and down her back.

I don't know if it was the effect of the mushrooms or if her eyes truly absorbed some of the flames as she moved up and down my body. Either way, I knew she must feel how hard I was now, pressing into her soft abdomen as she ground herself against my thigh.

Bella threw back her head and howled as she opened her arms wide. Then, without warning she leapt into my arms, wrapping her legs around me. I don't know when the kiss began, but it was the best I'd ever had and it seemed endless, like this dance, and this wonderful night.

Though I had known her in other ways, my bestial form prevented us from such an exchange. Here around this bonfire amidst this wild gathering was our first kiss. I had never felt more alive.

The next several moments were a blur. We made our way inside the castle, falling against one wall or the next, all over each other. Up the stairs to my chambers, we laughed as we left our clothes along the way, stumbling over each other and kissing like fools.

Bella wore only her tunic and all that remained of my attire was my trousers as I sat her onto the dresser and stood between her legs.

"I think it's safe to say that tonight has gone well," I said, smiling as I kissed her again. "I am truly surprised it isn't the wolves that hunt *you*."

I don't know what made me say it, but I was instantly filled with regret when I saw the look in her eyes. She was clearly thinking of Wolf. *Now*, I should tell her. This was my moment.

"I need to tell you something," she panted. "I can't do this right now, not because I don't want you, because I do." She hesitated. "There is someone else, someone who at least deserves me to tell him what is going on before we go any further."

"I know."

She looked confused and surprised, so I quickly said, "I mean I understand. I'm not who you think I am."

"You are not Maroc d'Ulfric, retired werewolf hunter?" she said sarcastically. "Because I met him recently and you look *exactly* like him."

I couldn't help but laugh. "No, what I'm trying to say is that I'm also someone else. You see, I'm not only Maroc, but I'm also—"

"A werewolf!" Claude yelled, bursting into the room.

"What?" Bella and I asked together.

"*Monsieur*, there is a werewolf on the grounds outside. It is attacking the horses."

I slurred a string of curses as I stomped across the room toward my silver sword.

"I *love* horses."

"What are you going to do?" Bella called, quickly straightening her tunic. "You haven't fought a werewolf in five years."

As I unsheathed my sword I turned to her and spread my arms wide. "Does it look as though I've grown soft to you?"

She smiled wryly and her eyes drifted down my body suggestively. "No, quite the opposite. But I don't believe you mean to attack them with *that* particular weapon."

I pointed toward my closet. "There's a large trunk in there full of weapons. Choose something and follow me as fast as you can." I turned for the door, then looked back with a smile. "You might also want to locate your leggings."

Chapter Twenty Two

Maroc

Bella quickly grabbed a smaller silver sword and followed me out the door and down the stairs. She seemed completely unbothered by her state of undress, but just the same, I tossed her the leggings when I found them. She gave me a wry smile as she practically leapt into them. We moved quickly back through the castle, finding both of my boots at the foot of the stairs and only one of hers. As we entered the courtyard we found the second.

"At least I won't have to face werewolves with one fucking boot," she said.

This was far more entertaining to me than it should have been. I laughed uproariously before saying, "I am still very much under the effects of those mushrooms."

Bella smiled. "Your eyes look like they're glowing right now, so I'm certain I am as well."

Either that or my beast was beginning to show through. Oh, *merde*!

"I haven't used mushrooms since I've changed." It took me a moment to realize I'd said this out loud because of the look she was giving me.

"Are you up for this?" she asked.

I nodded. "I'm fine. I read that Viking berserkers used to eat hallucinogenic mushrooms before going into battle. Actually, being out of my mind on mushrooms might make fighting werewolves easier."

"It will certainly make it more interesting," she said.

Only a few of the villagers seemed to notice as we ran along the outskirts of those gathered in the courtyard. Most were in varying stages of undress and blissfully unaware of any danger.

"What's going on?" Islene asked as we passed her.

She was dancing with a well-built older man whom I recognized as a woodcutter, but didn't remember his name.

"Werewolves are attacking the stables. I don't know how many," I said to her.

"I'll come with you," the man said.

"Royce, you don't even have a weapon," Islene said. "Besides that, you are not the hunter, I am."

The way he smiled at her last statement showed how much he cared for her. Everything was clear to see in his eyes.

"Do you have an axe," he asked, turning his attention back to me.

"Lodged in a stump near the stables." I hadn't realized Claude was behind me until he spoke.

"You plan to walk out there unarmed until you reach the stables?" I asked him.

He shrugged. "It wouldn't be the most reckless thing I've ever done."

"Where are your weapons?" Islene asked me.

I turned and pointed behind us as I spoke. "Through those doors, up the stairs and down the left corridor. My chambers are the last door on the left, in the direction of the tower. Most of my silver weapons are in a large trunk in the closet."

"Be careful. I've grown fond of this one," she said, patting Royce's shoulder. "Don't wait for me. Hurry before anyone gets hurt."

I realized years ago that Islene LaCroix does not look or move like anyone else her age. But seeing her take off running with the speed of a small deer still gave me pause.

"You heard the woman, let's go," Royce said.

Claude remained near the front entrance with a short sword and two guards to keep the villagers in and, hopefully, werewolves out.

I heard a cry of anguish from one of the horses and started to run for the stables. To my surprise both Bella and Royce easily kept pace with me.

"Where are your guards?" Bella asked in a hushed tone.

"I don't employ many, and other than the two you just saw, they're out of their minds on mushroom laced wine."

"Perfect," Royce said.

"Can I ask why *you* aren't going wild with the rest of the crowd?" I said to him.

"I've been close to Islene for a long time. I'm a one sip man when it comes to her potions."

"So, the world looks more beautiful, but you don't feel like running through the woods naked or starting a conversation with a spider," Bella said.

"Exactly."

Normally I would have stopped below the slight hill just before the stables and tried to surprise the enemy. After an entire glass of "blessed" wine this did not occur to me. I supposed no one else made the suggestion for similar reasons.

At a glance I saw three werewolves, one dead horse, one man on the ground, and one stable hand fighting the monsters with a pitchfork.

Rage flooded my senses like a wave breaking against rocks.

"This is my home," I roared.

I charged headlong toward the closest beast, tripped on the entrails of the dead horse, and missed the werewolf entirely. Not only was I intoxicated and out of practice with a sword, I sorely missed my claws and teeth.

I regained my footing, looked up and saw that Royce now had an axe in hand. He took a swing at the werewolf nearest to the stable hand and chopped it right in the back. Before he could pull the axe out for another strike the wolf spun around to face him. Out of nowhere a sword appeared in the werewolf's chest. It took me a moment to realize that Islene had nearly caught up to us and threw the sword from several feet away.

The other two wolves ran to help, but between them, Islene, Royce, and Bella had the situation well in hand. As the head of one monster hit the ground I realized the man at my feet was not dead.

While the werewolves were not paying attention I dropped my sword and rolled the man over. Other than a gash on his forehead he appeared uninjured. I saw no bites or scratches.

There are not a great deal of survivors when it comes to werewolf attacks. Unless you include the victims of Bastian Cheney, the infamous Beast of Gévaudan. The majority of werewolves do not leave anyone alive, unless they are interrupted. Those who are turned are mostly deliberate. Accidents like myself are rare.

I quickly threw him over my shoulder and moved him to the back of the stables where I hoped he would be safe. I turned to find a large male werewolf watching me.

"What the fuck are you doing?" he growled. "I can smell the difference in you. Why are you helping *them*?"

Not every werewolf could detect the difference in my scent and until now it had never been an issue. Perhaps it was because of the potion? Was I *not* completely human in appearance right now? A partial transformation might change my scent. I had to be careful. If I touched my sword anywhere but the leather-covered hilt while transformed, partially or otherwise, smoke would rise from my skin. This would give me away, even if only my eyes had turned.

I stepped away from the unconscious man and looked around quickly for a weapon.

"Looks like I'm going to be fighting you with a riding crop," I said, picking it off the saddle near me. "This should be interesting."

"Wait," the werewolf said. "You're *him*, the Comte d'Ulfric. You're a fucking werewolf!"

"Keep your voice down."

I lunged forward and struck him across the chest with the riding crop.

He laughed. "And no one knows," he said. He flexed his clawed hands as if preparing for some kind of exercise. "This is information my alpha will find most useful. Might even grant me some *mercy*."

"Except for the fact that you aren't leaving here alive."

I cracked him across the thigh as I rushed past and he howled. "You hit my balls, you filthy cunt!" he roared.

"And that is why I wear trousers," I said to myself.

I turned in time for his jaws to snap alarmingly close to my throat. I hit him across the face with the crop several times before making another run for my silver sword.

A clawed hand caught me around the ankle just as I located my weapon. I slid through the still warm blood and viscera of the poor dead horse once again. Only this time I did so on my face.

I fought to rake the guts from my face and see what was going on, but the werewolf was on my back. He shoved my face into the entrails as if trying to drown me. I needed a weapon. I couldn't let them see what I am. Especially Bella, not like this. I wanted to talk to her first. But I needed my claws.

My fingernails extended, slicing into the blood covered earth beneath me. I pushed up and thrust back with my hips, throwing the werewolf off balance enough for me to flip over beneath him.

I stabbed him in the ribs with my claws, over and over again, as fast as I could. He howled and put a big hand over my throat, squeezing tight. I drew back as much as possible from my position and punched him in the cock.

He howled in pain and as he fell forward onto me, I grabbed him with my thighs, flipping us over.

I still couldn't reach my sword. I grabbed the closest thing I could find and began to strangle him with it. Unfortunately for us both, it was the intestines of the horse. The werewolf was incredibly strong and the only way I could hold him was to unleash a part of my own beast.

My eyes burned, letting me know they were now wolf amber as my night vision became clearer. I dug my heels into the ground, thrusting my hips upward and cranked back on the string of intestines as hard as I could. I wrapped them tighter around my hands as the werewolf gasped for air.

"Stab him," I yelled. "Stab him before they tear!"

I didn't need to elaborate on what "they" were as I assumed all those present could clearly see I was strangling a werewolf with horse intestines.

"Wolf?"

Bella's softly spoken question startled me so badly that the werewolf I'd been wrestling nearly escaped my hold.

As she stared down at me wide-eyed, I realized my voice had deepened with my partial transformation and she'd recognized it.

Careful to make my voice sound normal I said, "Bella, I can't hold him much longer."

Not to mention I couldn't let him return to his alpha with the knowledge of what I am. If this alpha truly was Gaston Cheney, brother of the infamous Beast, there's no telling how he would use such information. No one needs a raging lunatic alpha who dabbles in the occult knowing their secrets.

I needed the wolf within to restrain this monster, but the instant Bella penetrated his chest with my silver sword, I reigned in my beast.

The werewolf howled in agony. I rolled from beneath him and Bella put all of her weight into the hilt of the sword, pushing forward. With a slushing crunch the blade sunk to the hilt in his chest, pinning him to the ground.

The werewolf made one last awful gurgling noise. He reached for her, but Bella took one step back. She resumed staring at me with his bloody grasping fingertips only inches from her face.

Chapter Twenty Three

Belladonna

"Are you all right?" Maroc asked me.

I found that I couldn't reply. All I seemed capable of was staring, looking for some trace of what I saw before.

"Bella?" he said softly, rising from the gore around him. "What is it?"

Maroc opened his mouth again, but it was Royce who spoke. "That damned wine was more potent than I thought. For a moment there, I thought *you* were turning into a werewolf."

Royce laughed and Maroc gave me an uneasy smile.

I took a deep breath, stepped away from the impaled werewolf, and then I laughed as well.

"I'm hallucinating," I said at last, shaking my head.

I looked up to find Maroc towering over me. How did he get so close without making a sound?

He was covered in blood, his hair in wild disarray, and somehow … he was beautiful. I looked him in the eyes as I said, "Do me a favor?"

"Anything."

"No mushrooms at our wedding. *None*." The last I added with a glance at my grandmother who merely shrugged.

Maroc laughed. "I swear it."

As we stepped farther away from the carnage he asked, "What *would* you like to be served at the wedding?"

"I don't care if it's cocks on a stick, just as long as there are no mushrooms in sight."

He laughed hard enough to let me know he was still feeling the effects of the blessing potion also.

"That's not true," I said. "I refuse to eat cock on a stick."

*****

"No one even noticed the blood," Maroc said to me.

He'd returned to the revelry to take the stable hands inside.

"They must feel like the luckiest men alive," he said.

"Where is my grandmother?"

"In the kitchen, drinking water with the woodcutter. I think he's trying to sober up before going home. This party will likely rage until morning."

"When it will be safer for everyone to be on the road."

He nodded. "You could stay," he said softly.

"I am covered in blood."

He smiled down at me. "I have a bathtub."

"That you also need to use."

"I have more than one."

I couldn't help but laugh. "I've already called for Samson. He will be here soon."

"And you never disappoint your horse?"

"Never." I put a hand against his bare chest, feeling how fast his heart still raced. "Maroc, there are things I need to think about. We have a serious werewolf problem that needs to be dealt with *soon*. Once she's finished seeing Royce safely home, I'm sure my grandmother will want to discuss plans with me."

"I can help."

"No," I said. My reply was softly spoken, but firm. "Although I doubt anyone else could strangle a werewolf with horse guts, you've retired. I respect that. Everyone should have that right when they've had enough. After losing your father, I understand." I patted his chest. "Stay safe and make the preparations for our wedding, because I wouldn't know a dinner fork from a tuning fork."

The rumble of his deep laughter was nearly enough to change my mind about staying.

"Our conversation in my chambers," he said softly. "I was trying to tell you something."

"Yes. What I mentioned to you is one of the things I need to think about."

"But, Bella, I am—"

"Missing!"

I looked around Maroc's muscular body to find Cherry running toward us. She looked as if she'd been crying.

"Perrin is missing," she gasped, stopping beside Maroc.

"I didn't expect him to come to a celebration of my engagement since we used to—" With a sharp look from Maroc I changed the course of my reply. "Why would you assume he is missing?"

"I was in the kitchen just now with Royce and Islene." She paused to take another deep breath. She'd obviously run all the way from the kitchen, on the back side of the castle.

"Perrin was delivering oak chests to Pomme de Terre, some specialty pieces he made himself. Royce thought he decided to stay a few extra days at The Salted Pork, which is nothing unusual for him."

"Especially since you've been carrying on with Armand," I said dryly.

Cherry looked near tears again. "Don't say this is my fault. I couldn't bear it."

"That's not how I meant it," I said softly, reaching for her hand. "Now, tell us what was said."

"It wasn't anything specific, I just have a *feeling*. Royce said that after what happened tonight, if Perrin wasn't back by tomorrow night, he would go looking for him the next day."

"Who is he to you?" Maroc asked gently. "Both of you, and be honest."

"He was supposed to be my lover, but I've been unfaithful," Cherry said bluntly. "But he is still my childhood friend and I care deeply for him, no matter who I am bedding."

Maroc's eyes widened at her forward response, but he said nothing as he turned his attention to me.

"He was once my lover as well and I've known him since I was a child. I'll tear the cock off of anyone who has done him harm."

His mouth turned up slightly. "What if he's been harmed by a woman?"

"Tits, cock, something is getting torn off if Perrin has been hurt."

Maroc opened his mouth and I believe I surprised us both by putting a finger over his lips. "I think I know what you are about to say, and you would stand out far too much to go roaming around Pomme de Terre or asking questions in a tavern."

He raised one dark brow and slowly removed my finger from his lips. "And a famous huntress will *not* draw attention?"

Cherry cleared her throat loudly. "Please don't dismiss me for saying so, Comte, but Bella will not draw the same *kind* of attention."

He seemed fairly amused. "And what kind of attention is that?" he asked.

"Aside from most folks around here knowing you are very wealthy?" She blushed. "The kind of attention drawn by a nearly seven foot handsome giant," she said.

He smiled broadly. "You think I'm handsome?"

"I think you are beautiful," I said honestly. "And you stand out far too much in a crowd. People will also be less likely to talk to someone in a position of authority."

"Do you think my father and I never stopped at taverns when we hunted all those years?"

"And what kind of attention did you draw?" Cherry asked shrewdly.

"Mostly women of a particular nature."

She and I both laughed.

"There is no reason to assume that Perrin is in any kind of danger, other than drowning in ale. Let Cherry and I sort this out. That is, if she can have another day off?"

He nodded slowly, a smile still curving his sensuous mouth. "I *do* have dead werewolves to clean up," he said. "I don't dare ask for help and have everyone more afraid than they already are. I've asked the young men from the stables to keep silent. They have seen enough for one night."

"Are you and Claude really going to tackle that mess alone?" I asked.

"I'd say that goes beyond the normal services of a valet," Cherry said.

"We also have a horse to bury. I should get started."

He looked from one of us to the other as Samson galloped up behind me. "You may as well leave with her tonight. Get an early start," he said to Cherry.

"Please tell your seamstress I won't be back in time to meet with her tomorrow evening," I said as I swung up onto Samson's broad back. "The seamstress in the village, Janette, has a list of all my measurements. I'm certain she'll be glad to share them."

He nodded again. "Do you always take charge?" he asked.

In one move he gripped Cherry's narrow waist and lifted her onto the horse behind me.

I smiled down at him with a wink. "Always."

Chapter Twenty Four

Belladonna

I barely slept. The more I thought about the events of that evening the more convinced I was of what I saw. But more than anything, *I knew that voice.* Not to mention, Royce and I would not have had the exact same hallucination. Not only was Maroc a werewolf, I believed he was *my* Wolf.

"But if this is true, why not tell me now?" I wondered aloud.

Perhaps *that* is what he was trying to tell me last night. Still, a nagging voice inside my head reminded me that I might have heard Wolf's voice because I was thinking about him. I was also under the considerable influence of Islene's damn potion.

Royce may *not* have witnessed the *exact* same things I did, but merely something similar. We were looking at werewolves. It would not be unusual for the mushrooms to make us see or hear more of the same. There were too many variables to be certain.

"Damn," I said, nearly spilling my cup of tea.

Cherry groaned and stirred beneath the furs on my bed. She sat up and squinted at me where I sat with a book I was too distracted to read, by the light of a lantern.

"When you said we'd get an early start, I didn't think you meant before dawn. Have you even slept?"

"I dozed for a few minutes in this chair."

"Are you that worried about Perrin? Do you think something terrible has happened to him?"

"No," I said softly. "I was thinking about something I saw last night. Trying to sort out if it was real or not."

She scoffed and pulled the blankets up to her chin. "I'm going to guess that whatever it was, it wasn't real. Remember my rabbit ears?"

I laughed softly.

"Let me sleep until dawn," she said. "Then, I'll feel much better once we track Perrin down."

"So will I. I'm sure he's fine."

*****

Shortly after daybreak Cherry and I sat out for Pomme de Terre on Samson. She borrowed some of my clothes and the blush of shame seemed permanently burned into her pale cheeks.

"You can see *everything*," she said, again straightening her cloak in an attempt to hide her body.

"Since when have you ever been shy?"

"Since I've never gone out in public with my lady parts on full display."

I shrugged. "You get used to it."

"These leggings are comfortable though."

*****

We found out that Perrin made it safely to the shop where his deliveries were received. We knew a few other places he liked to stop when he was in Pomme de Terre. All of the people we spoke to *had* seen him, but didn't know where he was at the moment. Several assumed he'd already left the village for home.

Since a lot of people recognized me, even without my red cloak, they offered other information as well. Two local men were missing. They hadn't been seen in a week which was unlike either of them. With recent events folks were quick to assume that werewolves were involved. So, they told me every detail they thought might possibly lead to my grandmother and I finding and slaying more monsters.

"This village has been safe for a long time. It's depressing to think we might be fucked again, after all these years," the barkeep said.

After searching until sunset, we'd at last made our way to The Salted Pork. We would have started there, except they didn't open until dusk. There were only a few patrons when Cherry and I arrived. One of which sat at the far back table and was nearly hidden in shadows.

He was very large, wearing a dark cloak and hood that he never removed, and a mask that seemed to cover his face entirely. That is, judging by what little I could see of him without outright staring.

The most disturbing detail we'd found was that Perrin's horse and cart were still in the stables behind the tavern. At least, *I* found this disturbing because it wasn't like him to just leave his horse, let alone any belongings he might have brought with him.

"I've been keeping his mare fed," the barkeep said, bringing my attention back to him.

"When did you last see him?" Cherry asked.

The man paused, stroking his red beard as if deep in thought. "Five nights ago. If you stay for a while, some of the locals might know more."

"Was he here with anyone?" I asked.

He shrugged. "I only remember how much he drank that night." He laughed. "Didn't expect him to turn up for a day or two after that. But by the third day, I started to worry." He nodded his head toward the dark stranger in the corner. "*He* was here that night. Perhaps you should ask if he's seen your friend."

Cherry gave the man in the corner a nervous glance. "Is it safe to talk to him?"

The barkeep laughed. "He's big but I don't think he'd harm a lady. He comes in about once a month or so. Drinks the strongest liquor I've got and never causes a problem."

"Does he always wear a mask?" I asked.

"He does. Some of us have guessed at the reasons for that. Personally, I think he might be disfigured in some way. Some of the women here have tried to talk him into taking it off, but so far nothing has worked. Not even when Bessie flashed her magnificent tits."

A barmaid to our right, who must be Bessie, smiled at the compliment.

I laughed and nearly choked on ale. "How did he respond?"

He laughed again. "He flashed his chest right back at her, but he kept on that bloody mask."

Cherry laughed then too.

"He sounds like someone whose company I might enjoy," I said. "What's his name?"

"We call him Stranger."

Chapter Twenty Five

Maroc/Wolf

When I saw Bella walking toward me through the gathering crowd, I wondered if I'd made the right decision in coming here. I came to The Salted Pork tonight hoping to see her, to watch over her, because I knew eventually their search would bring them this way.

I stopped by about once a month, using a soft leather mask and a partial transformation to hide my identity. Only my eyes and mouth were visible and the one woman who had looked closely enough to know those in either form was getting closer by the second.

My eyes were amber and lined with dark kohl. My voice I allowed to fully change and I increased my height, stopping the transformation just before my feet began to turn into paws. I also had slightly more body hair than usual, but that was all concealed beneath my clothing that I did not intend to remove.

I originally started coming to The Salted Pork after my father died to listen for rumors about werewolf sightings. I didn't intend to come out of my early retirement, but I *did* want to be as certain as I could be that Gaston's pack was dead. I now believed the she-wolf I killed recently was the remaining pack member that was unaccounted for over the past five years.

However, Bella and Cherry are correct; people are more guarded around nobility, or anyone they perceive to have authority. Even if you are or were a werewolf hunter. So, in order to test my transformation abilities, I practiced until I could turn just enough to not entirely look like myself. I added the mask and cloak and this is the only way anyone at The Salted Pork ever sees me.

"Can I join you?" Bella asked, offering me another mug of liquor.

I nodded and she sat across the small round table from me. Her long red hair spilled over one shoulder as she leaned forward, contrasting beautifully with the dark green of her cloak.

My heart was beating so fast I felt lightheaded. The moment I spoke she would know me. *"What will happen then?"* I wondered. *"Did she see more than I thought last night or does she believe whatever she saw was the due to the mushrooms?"*

She watched me for a moment, sipping her ale and not saying a word. When I reached for the mug she took my hand. The warmth of her touch seeped through the supple leather of my gloves. When she smiled, I knew our game was at an end.

"What beautiful amber eyes you have, *Stranger*."

"The better to see you in this dimly lit tavern."

Her smile was triumphant as she leaned across the table. She moved slowly, with the grace of a cat. I thought my heart was going to beat through my chest when she opened my cloak and pressed her face against my chest.

She breathed deeply and sighed. "I'd know that scent anywhere, even if your eyes and voice hadn't already given you away. What are you doing here, Wolf?"

Bella looked as if she had more to say, but reconsidered and sat back down across from me.

I glanced behind her and saw Cherry watching us with an expression of horror mixed with confusion.

"By the reaction of your friend I'm guessing you don't greet everyone this way."

She smiled and waved at her friend, but Cherry looked less than reassured.

Bella took a long drink and leaned back in her chair, crossing her legs and drawing my attention to the tight crotch of her leggings in the process.

"You must think I'm incredibly stupid," she said with a laugh.

"No, I—"

"This," she said, gesturing between us, "will have to wait."

"Are you sure about that?""

She looked me up and down suggestively. "I am certain that I know who you are now. But I'd like for you to wait to confirm my suspicions. Wait until a moment where you feel I would enjoy the revelation most." She winked. "You have no idea how much this gets me wet. But I am here for other reasons tonight. So for now, you are Wolf or Stranger as they call you, and you may be able to help me find my friend."

"If your friend is missing, why do you keep smiling?"

"This means I don't have to stop fucking you now."

I laughed, feeling both relieved and very aroused. *"Were* you planning to stop fucking me?" I asked.

"If you're not who I think you are, I should."

"That's not an answer."

"No, it isn't."

I sighed and tried to hide how hard I was by adjusting my cloak. "If it excites you, I can be anyone you wish."

The way she squirmed in response let me know that was exactly the right answer.

"Tell me about the friend you mentioned. How can I help?"

"His name is Perrin and he was here four or five nights ago. Apparently, so were you. He's my age, tall, short dark hair, blue eyes, very handsome."

I growled.

"Don't be jealous," she said playfully. "Did you see him when you were last here?"

"I might have. I'm sure you understand when I say I wasn't paying close attention to handsome young men."

She smiled again and a thrill ran through me.

If I had realized the man she was looking for, I could have been completely honest and perhaps saved her a trip. But, I'd never met Perrin and it didn't occur to me last night to ask what he looked like.

"A man who meets his description was very drunk that night. The tavern was full and I wouldn't have noticed except he kept trying to dance on the tables."

"That sounds like Perrin."

"The last time I saw him he was drinking with a beautiful woman who looked like a gypsy."

She nodded and sighed with what appeared to be relief. "Chances are he is still enjoying himself and will return home within a few more days. You could tell if she was a werewolf, couldn't you?" she asked.

"They passed right by my table and she did not smell like a werewolf."

Bella sighed again. "Well, that's settled then. Knowing my engagement celebration was taking place soon, he probably decided to stay here a while. We were once closer than we are now."

"Are you *trying* to make me jealous now?"

Her smile was wicked. "I like it when you growl."

"I'll keep that in mind."

"Why do they call you Stranger?"

"Is this what we're doing?" I thought. *"Well, if I'm going to continue to play the role, then let's play, Bella."* I had to admit, this excited me as well. "I'm afraid that's not a very interesting story. The barkeep asked me, 'What should I call you,

stranger?' and I said that Stranger was good enough for me."

I paused, watching her reaction before deciding to continue. Even though I was certain she knew my true identity, if it got her hot to think of me as Wolf, I intended to stoke that fire.

"Now that you've finally seen him, what do you think of your betrothed?"

"I think he is full of surprises." She laughed softly and took another sip of ale. "I'm actually very relieved. I wish I'd met him sooner. It's my own fault and stubbornness that may have cost us some good years."

I shook my head and finished my drink in one big gulp. "Those years made you the woman you are today. Never regret, it will rob you of more time. Tell me, will you dress like a woman for your wedding?"

She opened her cloak, revealing her leather corset and array of silver knives.

"If you like the way I look in leather, you should see me in lace," she purred.

Chapter Twenty Six

Belladonna

"My friend and I should be on our way. I think it's safe to say that Perrin doesn't want to be found. Even though I don't need your protection, I find it endearing that you're trying to watch over me, *Wolf*."

I stood slowly, watching the way his eyes burned brighter as his hungry gaze raked over me.

"I'm going to check on Perrin's horse and cart, make sure he hasn't been robbed. Then, I'll be going."

I had a quick word with Cherry, letting her know I would return shortly.

"Oh, I should finish my drink," she said.

Cherry is not a fast drinker.

"That's why I'm letting you know now."

"And what did the big stranger have to say?" she asked.

I leaned close to her and whispered, "That's Wolf."

Her eyes widened. "He doesn't look like a werewolf from here."

"He isn't right now, but he's not entirely human either. He's something in between." Something incredibly lust-worthy.

"So, you know who he is then?"

I almost told her, but it was not my secret to share. "He's wearing a mask, but I know his voice, and his scent."

She raised a brow. "His scent?"

"If you got close enough, you'd understand."

"I think across the room is close enough. He scares me."

I laughed softly. "Of all the things to be afraid of, Wolf is not one of them, trust me."

I walked into the large stables behind the tavern and found Perrin's mare easily enough. She recognized me and greeted me with a bump of her nose. I stopped to stroke her neck, speaking a few soft words of greeting. She seemed well cared for.

Perrin's cart was in the middle of the stable. His supplies were still neatly packed and stored underneath the seat.

"I hope you are enjoying yourself, and you are safe, "I said softly.

I was about to walk away from the cart when a large warm body pressed against me from behind.

I shivered as Wolf bent down and growled in my ear. His arms wrapped tightly around me and I reached up to stroke his muscular forearms.

"Are you here to confirm your identity to me?" I asked.

"No. You told me to wait until you would enjoy it most." His deep laughter rumbled against my throat as he kissed me. "I believe I can do better than this."

"Then why did you follow me?"

He took my hand and held it behind my back as he pressed his long hard length into my palm.

"To give you this thick wolf cock," he growled in my ear.

I smiled as I stroked him. "What if someone sees us? The stable doors are wide open."

"Let them watch. They might learn something."

He pulled my cloak aside as he nipped gently against the back of my neck. His fingers slipped beneath the edge of my corset and the next thing I knew my arse was bared to the cold night air.

With my leggings around my knees he spread my legs only wide enough to run his hand between my thighs. I wasn't wearing any pantalettes.

"I see you took the gloves off."

"The better to stroke your slick little pussy," he rumbled.

"Are you going to just fuck it right here, up against this cart? I think I'm too short for that."

"I can bend down. All you need to do is hold onto me."

I reached back and braced my hands against his rock hard thighs. He stroked my clit from the front in slow deliberate circles as he used his other hand to guide his cock inside me. I gasped. He stretched me to the limit and began to slowly pump into my wetness.

"I don't want to ride home with a dripping cunt," I gasped as he slammed into me.

"Then I'll pull out," he groaned, thrusting deeply. "I just had to have a quick dip in that tight little slit. Just thinking about it is enough to make me so hard it hurts."

The sounds of our breathing and wet flesh slapping together echoed in the silence of the stables.

"You think you can just take this pussy whenever you want it?"

I reached into the pocket of my cloak and pulled out part of the thin silver chain. Smoke rose like steam from his exposed forearm as I pressed the chain against his skin. His growl sounded more aroused than filled with pain.

"I'll take what I like, because it is mine."

My juices gushed down my thighs in response.

"Then fuck it like you own it," I commanded.

I moaned as he thrust harder, biting my lip to try to keep quiet. "When you pull out, try not to come on Perrin's cart."

His laughter was deep and wicked as he mercilessly pounded into my pussy.

"I should," he said. "I should come all over it, assert my dominance."

My pussy clenched and Wolf held me tight, slamming into me as I came on him. I cried out with a mixture of pleasure and pain. He moved faster and his big hand closed over my mouth.

He whispered, "If you scream, someone will *definitely* catch us fucking in the stables."

My cries were only partially silenced by his palm. My muscles continued to pulse around his thick cock. The way he was working my clit, I found that my release would not stop.

I continued to come even after he pulled out of me. I stood there for a moment, bare arse out, gasping for air as I rested against the side of the cart.

"Well, that was unexpected."

"Do I hear a complaint?" he teased.

"No *monsieur*, not from me."

I watched him watching me straighten my clothes.

"You could stay the night," he said softly.

"I can't. As much as I would love to smother myself in your chest hair, I should get back to my grandmother."

"Is she all right?"

"She is anxious to have one more hunt before the wedding. She talks about it as if this might be her last, which worries me."

"Is she in good health?"

"Never better. She said she has a bad feeling about this hunt, but needs to be done with it."

"Hmmm." The sound of his low rough voice contemplating my question sounded almost like a growl and it made me shiver again. I watched him, standing in the shadows, his amber eyes glowing brightly beneath the black mask. By the gods I could jump him again.

"Does she perform divination?" he said after a moment's pause. "Perhaps your grandmother knows something we do not."

"Oh, she knows plenty of things that I do not. She said last night that she feels this hunt will *settle* something, like a chapter in her life is nearing completion and she is ready to be finished with it. I'm not sure what that means, but it frightens me."

Wolf opened his arms, spreading his cloak to reveal the tight black clothing he wore underneath. He was sitting on a barrel though his legs were so long that his feet still reached the ground. As I walked closer he spread his legs so I could stand between his muscular thighs. I leaned into his warmth and was wrapped in his arms and heavy cloak. I slid my arms around his waist and sighed.

"This feels so good. I could hide here inside this cloak, against this magnificent body, and never see another soul."

"Magnificent?" he asked.

I smiled and forced myself to pull back from him, if only slightly. With very little effort I could lose myself entirely to his embrace. The gentle strength in his touch, his scent, and the warmth of his big body, they were like a siren's song.

He pulled me tightly against him again and I didn't stop him. His heart beating steadily beneath my ear was a sound I never knew I was missing.

"Take me with you," he said softly.

"Tonight?"

"On the next hunt." When I looked up at him he clarified, "I'll go as Wolf. I believe I can help."

"I'll ask my grandmother, but I feel fairly certain she will welcome the assistance."

"How will I know your answer?"

"Meet me at the edge of the forest that surrounds our home three days from now, just before the sun sets. She wants to leave at dusk."

"If she feels such urgency, why wait three days?"

"That's how long it will take to finish the potion she's brewing."

"She's brewing a potion to fight werewolves?"

I shrugged. "I admit this is something new for me. We've used potions, but not ones intended as weapons. She said it will be worth the wait."

"Bella," he said softly. "I'm falling in love with you."

"Good," I said, fighting the emotions tightening my throat, "because I am *definitely* falling in love with you."

His lips were soft and warm and his gentle kiss held a promise of things to come. I pulled back from him again and forced myself to withdraw from his embrace.

"Keep the mask," I said. "I like it."

Chapter Twenty Seven

Gaston

"People are not as fond of their fingernails as you might think," I said. "It's not until you get down to the meatier bits that they really start to beg."

The woman wept, but she did not beg. Not yet.

I leaned against the wall where she was chained. Only one of our previous captives remained and he was to be part of tonight's ritual. He was tied to a chair on the far side of the large chamber in order to give him a better view of the ceremony.

I sighed. "How about I tell you what I already know and you can fill in the gaps in my knowledge?" I asked her.

She glanced nervously toward our other captive.

"Do you know him?"

"Yes."

"Ah. We're getting somewhere. *How* do you know him?"

She hesitated.

"Is it worth losing another fingernail?"

"He comes to the tavern where I work."

"Jules tells me you were near the stables outside of The Salted Pork when he found you."

"Jules?"

I nodded toward the fully transformed werewolf across from me. He was currently devouring half of a deer. Her obvious horror and revulsion made me smile.

"I didn't realize it had a name," she said.

"Watch your mouth, bitch," Jules growled.

Blood and viscera clung to his face and when he spoke the woman gagged.

"Oh. You're going to be a delight," I said. "What is your name?"

"Bessie."

"Tell me, Bessie, with werewolves loose in the countryside, what could possibly make you walk outside alone at night?"

She visibly struggled to form words.

"So, we've finally arrived at the heart of the matter. You see, Bessie, there is powerful magic at work here, preventing you from telling me exactly what I need to know. But if you can push beyond the pain and tell me anything of value, *anything* at all … I might let you live."

The glimmer of hope in her eyes was pathetic.

"I was refilling pitchers of ale in the kitchen when I thought I heard a scream."

"Jules also told me he overheard you talking to someone in the tavern about a werewolf hunter."

Her eyes widened as she looked at my beta wolf again.

"I don't always look like *this*, fool. I was in the tavern, heard you mention one of them, and so I followed you. The stables reeked of sex and werewolf."

She seemed surprised.

"It probably smelled good to you," I explained. "The stronger the werewolf, the better we smell. The scent is something our bodies produce naturally, like a fine cologne."

I shoved my chest into her face and when she tried to recoil I laughed. "Smell me."

She still struggled.

"She has two fingernails left," Jules said.

She stopped squirming and took a deep breath. "You smell very good," she admitted.

I took a step back. "Do you recall the smell in the stables?"

She nodded.

"Did it smell like me?"

Bessie hesitated only a moment before saying, "It smelled a bit like you, only better."

I growled and she tried to back away, but being chained to the wall, there was nowhere for her to go.

"That smell is why I looked around the stables. It was so strong, I thought someone must be near and I was certain I heard a scream. But all I found was *him*."

"Look at me like that one more time and I will tear out your eyes," Jules growled.

"She's got more courage than the men we've questioned, that's for certain," I said.

"Or she's stupid," he quipped.

"When the huntress finds you, I hope she cuts off your cock and shoves it down your throat," she spat at him.

Jules lunged for her, but I put out a hand to stop him as I laughed.

"That's it," I said.

Jules gave me a confused look and I nearly slapped him. I gestured to Mercy, casting a circle behind us. "She told us there is always a crack, even in the best armor. It's *anger*. The others we've questioned were all terrified and couldn't even say *half* of what she's already told us. No one else has even been able to mention that the hunter we seek is a woman."

"Well, the one man mocked you when he realized it. Actually, I don't believe he knew anything about them at all."

I turned back to Bessie. "But look at you. You're not broken. You're furious. And that anger is somehow allowing you to speak. What does she look like, this huntress?"

I knew the years would have changed her as they had me, so I wasn't looking for the vixen my brother once described. But from the pieces I had heard and been able to recall, she sounded like a fierce warrior despite her age.

Even posing the question was difficult for me to say aloud. But Mercy was working on the final spell. Soon the last stronghold of her magic would be broken and we would be able to find her.

"Red hair," she said through gritted teeth.

"Old?"

A fine sweat broke out on her face as she tried to speak, but no words came out. I slapped her, leaving a big red handprint across her face. Her eyes practically burned with rage.

"Young," she managed to say.

"And she's fucking an alpha werewolf," I mused aloud.

"Do you think she's working with him or just fucking him?" Jules asked. "Because there is definitely a werewolf out there killing pack members."

"I'm not sure that matters anymore." I focused on her again. "Did you see the man she was with?"

"We call him Stranger. He's big, but I've never seen his face. He wears a mask. They were talking before she left. Not sure if that's who she screwed in the stables or not."

"What about the older one? I've heard there are two." My skin burned and my eyes ached, but I forced myself to speak about her.

"I've never met her," she replied, visibly struggling as well.

Bessie's eyes widened suddenly and from the sounds coming from behind me, I knew the ritual had fully begun.

I turned around to watch. Mercy stepped into the middle of the large circle and as the werewolves around her began to transform, she let her robe fall to the floor. She turned her face up toward the sky, visible through the large hole in the ceiling. The chamber echoed with the sounds of bones breaking and reforming mingled with snarls, howls, and tearing flesh.

"They're not all the same," Bessie said weakly.

I looked back to her and it took me a moment to understand what she meant. "We all transform differently. Some of us shift from human to beast more *poetically*. Others grow impatient with the process and choose to tear their way out of their human skin."

She stared in horror, yet could not seem to look away. Mercy began speaking her incantation. I heard the witch moan and I smiled as Bessie's expression changed. Now, she was afraid.

"That's all right," I said softly. "Soon you'll be able to tell me everything. Whether you're afraid or not. Most people *beg* me for mercy, but she is the only mercy I have. That's her name," I explained. I gestured behind me to the witch who was now being fucked by two of my wolves at once. "Remember, do not scratch her," I called with a glance in their direction. "She needs your energy and your seed, not your curse."

Bessie looked as if she might vomit. I was enjoying her revulsion almost as much as the sounds of my witch being plowed by the entire pack.

"Well, tonight *everyone* is having Mercy. You see the young man in the corner, the one you recognized? He will be the final part of this ritual. The blood of someone who knows them must be spilled. Though he's been unable to say directly, I've gathered enough information to *know* that he's met the ones we seek. And that is enough. But first, the sacrifice has to watch."

I heard Mercy growl and I looked to see she had a werewolf on his back now. Instead of lying on her back and simply taking it, she was riding him like she intended to break him.

I turned my attention back to the barmaid. I wondered what would happen if I ripped off her last two fingernails while she watched them. I was getting hard from the sounds and smells of sex, but she'd started to cry.

"Fucking werewolves isn't for everyone," I sighed. "Does our other *guest* seem to be enjoying the performance as much as you are?"

To my surprise she began to laugh.

"Has your mind broken, woman?" I asked.

"He's gone," she said, laughing to the point of tears. "The chair is empty."

"Bastard," Jules growled. "He can't have gotten far."

"Let him go."

"What?"

I patted his furry shoulder. "I want the old bitch to know I'm coming for her. Besides, Bessie has seen at least one of them." I looked down at her and smiled as I began to transform.

"We have a new sacrifice," I said, my voice deepening as the beast took over. "Make sure she sees everything."

The barmaid's screams echoed in the night, mingling with howls and the sounds of my laughter.

Chapter Twenty Eight

Islene

I could feel The Beast's blood as only one contaminated by him could. If I've learned anything in my years as a hunter, it's that a wolf knows his or her master.

I wondered how such magic might work, since I killed the one who bit me. But now I know. There is no mistaking this feeling, this *call* within my blood.

The Beast is near, but I do not understand how. I *know* I killed him thirty four years ago, and Maroc d'Ulfric killed his brother five years ago. Actually, from what Maroc told me, his father and the werewolf nearly killed each other as Vallis died from his injuries a few days later. But it was Maroc who struck the final blow to the monster who took my friend's life.

He also said they killed the entire pack Gaston was currently leading, except for one who was, to my knowledge, never seen again. Even a wolf turned by The Beast should not feel like this, for I have known others. This feels like *him*, like Bastian. But that is not possible.

I was waiting on the porch for my potion to finish brewing and smoking a pipe packed with herbs when I saw Perrin running down the trail to my house.

At first I questioned which herbs I'd begun to smoke. But when I heard him call out to me I knew he was real and not a vision. As he came closer I saw that his tunic was open and bloody, his clothes torn, and he wasn't wearing shoes.

I ran to him, meeting him at the edge of our yard so quickly that it seemed to startle him. Now was not the time to be concerned with Perrin seeing abilities I usually kept hidden.

"What happened?" I asked.

He reached for me with trembling hands and I saw he was missing every single fingernail. I looked down at his bare feet and saw his toenails also appeared to have been savagely torn out, leaving some jagged pieces behind.

I took off my shawl and wrapped it around him. His handsome face had been badly beaten, but he would heal.

"A werewolf is coming for you," he said through chattering teeth.

"I know. Come, sit by my fire. Let me help you, Perrin."

"He's big and cruel, and he's not alone."

We began to walk toward the house with Perrin badly limping now that he'd stopped running. His feet were bruised and bloody.

"Lean on me," I said. "How far did you run?"

"Are you not hearing me, Islene? He's *coming*. He has a witch and they've been performing *rituals*. They said they would be able to find you soon. They were going to sacrifice me because I refused to tell them anything about you or Bella. They figured out that I knew you. Before I knew the witch was with them, I told her. She asked me directly if I knew the local hunters and I said yes. They said the sacrifice had to have met at least one of you."

I nodded grimly. "Even if they know exactly where I am, they cannot enter these woods. I promise you that. Come inside and let me clean your wounds before your father sees you. He's been worried."

As we started walking again I asked, "Any chance you could tell me his name, this big cruel werewolf?"

Perrin shook his head. "No. But he called the witch Mercy."

"Ah, Mercy Lavigne. It has to be. That explains a lot."

"How so?"

I helped him up the steps and onto the porch, cringing as I imagined how badly his feet must hurt.

"She would perform any manor of vile dark magic for the right price, and she likes to fuck werewolves. Our paths have crossed a few times. But until she breaks through my protective spells completely, I doubt she'll remember me at all."

*****

Much to my relief, after cleaning and bandaging Perrin's many injuries, he had not been bitten or cut deeply enough by claws to be changed.

"How did you run all the way from the outskirts of Pomme de Terre without anyone seeing you?"

While I worked he'd told me everything that happened since he left the tavern with Mercy, not realizing the danger he was in.

"After the mistake I'd already made, I hid in the woods, stayed off any road or open area."

I had his feet soaking in a mixture of herbs and he sighed when I added more warm water to the large pan. I hung the kettle back beside the fire to keep the remaining water heated.

"Bella and Cherry went looking for you two days ago."

He suddenly looked grief stricken. "They killed a barmaid I knew, Bessie, at least I assumed they were going to kill her. She mentioned someone looking for me when they questioned her. I only pray they did not find what found me."

"They've been back for some time. I didn't mean to leave that part out. I'm sorry. My mind is on this potion and what will surely be a hell of a fight."

Perrin nodded solemnly. "Where are they now?"

"Bella is out looking for someone who plans to join us on this hunt. Cherry has returned to her duties at the castle."

"I should speak with Cherry," he said. When I merely gave him a questioning look he continued. "She thinks I don't know she's been plowing Armand." Perrin laughed, then put a hand to his side as if the laughter caused him pain.

"You're not angry?"

He shrugged. "I never expected anything more from our relationship. If that is where her heart lies, so be it."

"You are as kind and forgiving as your father."

"Don't misunderstand. If I was in love with Cherry, I'd kill the cook and stuff him into a pie. But, the affection I feel for Cherry is not the same as it should be if you're going to spend your life with someone."

I patted his hand gently, careful to avoid his battered fingertips. "Spoken like a man with more sense than most. I have to prepare for tonight. I should have time to tell Royce where to find you. Then, we will set out at dusk. The potion is nearly done."

"You're going tonight?"

"Yes. And from what you've said, perhaps we should have found them sooner. We did try."

"I can go home. I'll be well enough."

I put a hand on his shoulder when he tried to stand. "No," I said gently. "If not for the cold your feet would already have infection. You are going to rest by this fire, drink what I've given you, and soak your feet." I handed him half a loaf of bread. "And eat something before you faint."

He tore into the bread ravenously. "I never thought I'd eat again after what they—" He stopped chewing and gagged.

"Don't think about it now, you need your strength. I understand what monsters are truly capable of. It is my goal tonight to end this once and for all."

"I counted nine werewolves, not including the witch and their alpha. I won't pretend to know what you're capable of, but I know you've been doing this for a long time. And you're good at it, because you're still alive."

Despite everything this made me smile. "They will have as much suffering as I am able to deliver, I promise you that."

"Good," he said darkly.

"I need to put this potion into bottles, pack my weapons, and meet Bella and her … companion. I will stop by your cabin on my way through the woods, but I must hurry."

"Thank you, Islene. My father will want to go with you when he hears about this. Please, don't let him."

*****

"Why?" Royce asked again. "I am strong and capable. And you said there are at least *ten* werewolves out there! *Merde*, Islene. Ten fucking werewolves."

I put my hands against his chest. I wanted to lean into his warmth, to kiss him and never leave.

"I am not going alone."

I didn't think I should tell him that we had a werewolf of our own to offer help tonight.

"Perrin will be fine, but he is terrified. Go to him. Stay at my house tonight. I will feel better knowing that neither of you are alone and that you are safe within my woods tonight."

"But Islene …"

"Because I love you," I said softly.

His blue eyes filled with tears as he looked down at me.

"You can't go, because I love you and I would lose what is left of my humanity if anything happened to you."

Royce kissed me so fiercely that it took my breath away.

"Then hurry home my huntress. This is not the last time I need to hear those words."

Chapter Twenty Nine

Cherry

Guilt over my unfaithfulness to Perrin has plagued me, particularly since he has not returned. Not to my knowledge anyway. He was last seen in the company of a woman. Perhaps that is a sign that I should be honest, apologize sincerely, and hope I have not ruined a lifelong friendship.

In fairness, we never professed to love one another in a romantic way. Our relationship grew more due to a physical attraction and a certain level of comfort with one another. Much like what happened between he and Bella and *they* remain friends.

Remembering this put my mind somewhat at ease. I could not say my present actions had the same effect. On our return ride from The Salted Pork Bella requested something from me. She asked me to sneak into the Comte's private chambers and look for a collection of books. Among these she asked that I search for a book about women (and perhaps men) copulating in various ways with werewolves.

"Why do you think he would have such a book?" I asked.

"If he does, it is the last bit of confirmation I need," she said.

"Of what?"

She laughed and said, "That Maroc d'Ulfric and I are a perfect match."

Normally, I would never risk my position at the castle for such a strange request, even from my dearest friend. However, I justified my decision to look for the book by the fact that I already borrowed texts from his library. *And* my friend would soon be his wife.

Why she could not wait until then to find out what is in his bed chambers, I do not know.

I overheard the Comte's valet, Claude, saying he had gone out riding and would not be back tonight for dinner. The kitchen staff had been told to enjoy their evening and he would return in time for breakfast.

So, having no fear of being discovered (by the Comte at least) I climbed the stairs to his chambers.

In the far back corner, across the room from his enormous bed, sat a bookshelf that reached from floor to ceiling. This immediately caught my attention because a portion of this bookshelf was open, like a door made of books.

Behind this open door was a set of winding stairs. I knew this must lead to the tower. I was told once that the tower was used for storage. Having never been in Comte d'Ulfric's chambers before, I never thought of the tower again.

But now, with the door wide open, my curiosity got the better of me. As I reached the door I heard a strange sound, like something sharp scraping against stone. Not feeling myself to be in any danger (foolishly) I quickly ran up the stairs and into the tower.

True to what I'd been told, the tower was filled with trunks and several more shelves of books. There was a desk with books and bottles of different sizes, a suit of armor, a rack filled with various weapons, and an expensive looking tapestry of a man fighting a whole pack of wolves.

Not far from this tapestry, between a bookshelf and the desk, was a large window. The shutters were open and a strong draft was blowing through. The cold wind was heavy with the scent of rain.

Since I work as a maid, my primary concern was that nothing in the tower should be damaged by rain. When I leaned out the window to grasp the latch on the shutters I happened to glance down. What I saw chilled me to the bone and sent me racing down the stairs.

I left the window and the door hidden in the bookshelf open. An enormous black werewolf was climbing down the tower! He was *leaving* the room, which means he was recently *in* the room. Since the entrance to the tower was hidden in his chambers that meant this werewolf *must* be the Comte! No one else was allowed in here and his valet was downstairs, so it could not be him.

I had to warn Bella! She confessed to me that she was already involved with a werewolf. If her soon-to-be-husband, who is apparently also a werewolf, were to discover them … Oh, this might go very badly for her. But how could I tell her?

I believe she is going on the hunt tonight and it is nearly sundown.

*****

I borrowed a horse form the stables and raced toward Bella's cottage. Perhaps I could reach her and warn her before she left.

It was foolish, what I was doing. But taking the main road, I had less of a chance of meeting any werewolves. Or so I imagined. And would Bella not risk herself for me?

At the edge of the forest that surrounds Islene's property I slowed to give the horse a rest. He'd certainly earned it. We made good time.

The sun was just setting, casting a beautiful orange glow over the landscape. Suddenly, I heard voices. My typical reaction to something like this is to keep moving. However, I recognized one of the voices as Bella. I tied the horse to a tree just off the road and crept closer.

I did not call out since it was clear she was not alone. I heard a very deep, and if I'm being honest, sultry, man's voice, but could not understand what he was saying.

I rounded a corner and saw Bella *and* Islene talking to the same werewolf I'd witnessed climbing from the tower!

I sank down behind some bushes and scarcely dared to breathe for fear of being discovered. I swear they were discussing *bonnets*.

The more I listened, though I could only understand an occasional word from this distance and in a high wind, it was clearly the Comte. His voice was deepened by the transformation, but to anyone who had heard him speak often, it was still clearly *him*.

Did they already know then? Was my interference completely unnecessary? I could certainly understand why Bella would choose to keep such a thing private, even from me.

Knowing her, she likely feels it is not her secret to reveal.

I peeked through the bushes and saw how close Bella was standing to him. Perhaps this was a game they were playing with each other?

When they started to leave I slowly backed away in the opposite direction. *Mon dieu!* I've been working for a werewolf. And was he wearing trousers?

Chapter Thirty

Belladonna

"If your reputation did not precede you, I'd never guess you were anyone's grandmother," Wolf said.

She agreed quite easily to accepting his help, asking only, "Do you trust him with your life?" When I replied that I did she said, "Then I shall trust him with mine."

As she looked at him now I wondered what biting retort she would make.

"Do you think I should be in bed knitting, wearing one of those ugly old bonnets?"

His deep laughter made me visibly shiver. I thought too late to conceal this reaction and caught him grinning down at me like a fiend.

"No," he said, turning his attention back to my grandmother. "I'd wager you don't even own a bonnet."

"I don't."

"Would you believe I do?" he asked.

To my surprise, even under our present circumstances, she laughed. "I like you, Wolf," she said, "but I'm afraid we must cut the pleasantries short and discuss our strategy for this hunt. We have some distance to cover as well."

He nodded. "I agree and if you'll hear me out while we travel, I have an idea."

Thanks to Perrin my grandmother knew the precise location of the rogue pack, which she then told us. She also knew we were up against at least ten werewolves and a witch. I felt like my heart was going to stop when she said *ten* werewolves. I swallowed my fear and chose to address something else first.

"That's exactly where the crystal pointed when I scryed for their location," I said. "We should have continued on."

"When we found those wolves farther south than we expected, there was no reason not to think they were the ones we sought," she said.

"Well, they were, just not all of them," I said.

"Besides, we had to bring the survivors back to the village," she added.

I was relieved to know he was safely back at our cottage, but still somewhat numb at learning what my friend had suffered. My grandmother didn't give a lot of details, which was probably for the best right now.

She'd walked into the woods, saw me standing beside a massive werewolf as if this were nothing unusual, and said, "Perrin is back. He escaped from the werewolves we are hunting. I know exactly where they are."

Through our brief conversation on the subject I learned he was tortured and he was nearly sacrificed by a witch named Mercy. It felt as if I'd been doused in ice cold water and my emotions were numb with the shock. So, I had put Perrin's ordeal out of my mind as best I could and introduced her to Wolf.

Rather than risk injury to our horses my grandmother and Wolf ran, both at an alarming speed, while he talked. He didn't even sound out of breath. In that moment I was reminded that I was the only one of us who was entirely human. I had never felt more vulnerable in my life and was unaccustomed to this type of fear.

Wolf carried me in his arms and the satchel of potions I'd brought was thrown over his shoulder. His body was too wide to wear the supplies on his back as I did. I listened as Wolf detailed a plan that was either brilliant or ridiculous, depending on how tonight would end.

However, my grandmother also shared many details, some of which I did not previously know.

"If their alpha is who I believe him to be, he has been hunting me for a long time," she said.

"And if he is who *I* believe him to be, we have some history as well. None of it good," Wolf said.

"And that is what makes you think this will work?" she asked.

"It is. He's so full of himself, I don't believe he will be able to resist. Are you agreeable to my plan then?"

I noticed neither of them actually said who they thought this mysterious alpha was, but they were talking so fast I couldn't get a word in to ask.

"It's better than what I had in mind," she said.

"Which was?" I asked.

"Cut their cocks off, stuff them up their asses, and drown the bastards in a river of their own blood."

She was joking, but only I knew that.

Wolf was so surprised by her response that he nearly tripped. "I think I understand you a little better now," he said to me, laughing softly. "Why do women keep threatening to cut off or tear off cocks?"

"Because that's one threat guaranteed to give a man pause," I said.

"We're getting close," she said.

My grandmother stopped and so did Wolf. "I will only use the invisibility spell on your cloak this time," she said to me. "Given what he has in mind it would be pointless if no one could see me. But you will be concealed until you attack, as before."

She pulled the small satchel from her back and handed me a thin vial of dark liquid. "This is part of my original plan that I still think we should use."

I held the vial up to the moonlight. "Is this blood?" I asked.

"Vampire blood."

"Where did you get vampire blood?" I asked.

She waved away the question. "That part is not important. What *is* important is this blood will help us to even the odds tonight. You both know that I am something other than human. *You* I've told. But after the way he has seen me run I think we can safely say Wolf has figured out I'm not simply a woman or a witch." She gestured to Wolf. "He is an alpha werewolf. And fearsome though you may be, my love, you are still human."

"You want me to *drink* this?"

"Yes, and the sooner the better. By the time we reach the ruins Perrin described the blood should be working."

"And you are telling me this *now*, right before a fight? You couldn't mention this sooner?"

I tried to ask more questions but she held up a hand to stop me.

"All of your senses will be enhanced. You will have increased speed and stamina. But most importantly, any injuries you might sustain tonight will heal at an inhuman rate. And if you are bitten by a werewolf, you will not turn. You cannot be contaminated by two monsters," she explained.

I couldn't tell by the look he gave her if Wolf was surprised or impressed. "Is that so?" he asked.

"Why did you not use this on hunts before?" I asked.

"Before I was bitten, I didn't know about such a use for vampire blood. As for you, I've been conducting some research before I'd give such a thing to my only living relative. I recently received some correspondence from a hunter in London who has successfully used vampire blood both to heal after a hunt as well as to prevent turning into a werewolf. You will *not* be permanently altered in any way," she assured me.

"If this is all true, why do more hunters not use it?" I asked.

"Because from what I understand it's like the mushrooms I put into the wine, not everyone can cope with the effects. Not to mention vampires don't exactly donate their blood to the cause."

When I paused she kept talking.

"The effects last for twenty four hours at most, could be less if you have a full stomach, or if you get sick after swallowing it. You might experience a short term aversion to silver. We're already wearing gloves in this cold, so it shouldn't be an issue. You would need to exchange blood with a vampire in a short amount of time in order to become one, so don't worry about that either."

When I still hesitated she asked, "Do you trust me, Bella?"

"I do, but I *will* have more questions later."

As I gulped down the blood she replied, "Pray to all the gods there is a later."

*****

By the time we reached the castle ruins I was not only running along beside them, I could match their pace.

"This is incredible," I whispered to my grandmother. "I can see in the dark, smell every creature in the forest, *feel* the night. Is this what it's like to be a vampire?"

"I'm sure it's all sweet meats and roses, until you burn to a crisp in the sunlight," Wolf said softly.

"That is a significant drawback," I agreed.

My grandmother passed me her bag and a few of her weapons. She had several concealed beneath her clothing, but this was more vulnerable than I'd ever seen her go into a dangerous situation.

Wolf reached out one large clawed hand to her and after a moment's hesitation she placed her hand in his.

"I swear to you, I have your back," he said.

"This is really the plan we're going with?" I asked.

They both shrugged and she replied, "It's not bad, if it works."

She quickly spoke the words over my cloak to make me invisible until I attacked before letting Wolf loosely bind her hands.

I hung back as I'd been asked to do, waiting until all attention was focused on them.

I leapt into a tree, alarmed by the noticeable increase in the height that I could jump. I remained still, afraid I might have already made too much noise. I could smell the werewolves lurking nearby. I had noticed the distinct scent of an alpha before, but I never knew that vampires could smell other, less powerful werewolves. I took a deep breath. Yes, there was no mistaking what my senses told me. A few of them were hiding out here in the woods and even like this, I could not see them.

I heard the sounds of growling and raised voices coming from the ruins. My emotions were on edge as I felt the night pulse with life around me and waited.

Chapter Thirty One

Islene

I walked behind the massive werewolf, following but not cowering. These monsters would *not* see fear in me.

They were gathered around a large fire, outside one of the old crumbling outer walls of the small keep. These ruins were often referred to as a castle, but they were truly dwarfed in comparison to Castle d'Ulfric.

Though he was introduced to me as Wolf, I strongly suspected it was Maroc d'Ulfric's broad back I followed through the gathering of snarling werewolves. When we were in his castle, in a crowd, it was easy to mistake his scent. Even when we went to the wine barrels he kept just enough distance between us that I simply thought he wore a strong, but intoxicating cologne. Being near him now however, that scent was unmistakable, at least to a werewolf hunter. Especially one like me.

Of all people *I* understood why he might hide his identity. If we survived this and he chose to tell me, that's fine. If not, that's fine as well.

I counted seven around us, but they kept their distance, allowing us to walk dangerously close to the man who must be their alpha.

"That's far enough," he called. His voice was smooth and commanding.

He remained on the far side of the fire from us, sitting on a gaudy sort of throne.

"Jules tells me you have a proposition, is that right?"

He gestured to a fully transformed werewolf to his right whom I assumed to be "Jules." He was the one who met us at the front of the keep and asked what business we had here. I believe the only reason he spoke to us rather than simply attack was because of Wolf.

So far I stayed back and let Wolf do all the talking, as was his plan. I even pretended to be restrained, but my hands were not truly bound. Before approaching the keep he'd smeared some dirt onto my face and loosened part of my braid, hoping to give the appearance of at least some small struggle between us. If they thought I was subdued, then perhaps they would not pay attention to me.

"I am here to challenge you to a fight," Wolf said.

Flames crackled and rose higher as the other alpha laughed. "To what end?" he asked.

"You are outnumbered and apparently not very smart."

"I challenge you, alpha to alpha, to a fight for this territory and this pack. If I win, your pack may leave, unharmed."

This drew more laughter from the pack.

"And when I win?" he asked.

"*If* you win, you can also have the gift I've brought you, because I won't be alive to stop you."

I'd left my tell-tale red cloak behind and though he no doubt *knew* someone was standing behind his challenger, I'm certain he did not recognize what little of me he saw. Especially since he had never seen me in person and only had descriptions from others that were clouded by my magic.

I stepped from behind Wolf and got my first good look at the man who'd been hunting me. His resemblance to Bastian was unmistakable. And in that moment I could see he recognized me as well.

"You are his brother."

He nodded slowly, moving around the fire to get a better look at me.

"Years ago I came back from Moldavia to share something with my brother, something I considered a gift. It never occurred to me that he was doing anything really stupid and keeping it from me. Like *fucking* a werewolf hunter on a regular basis."

As he came closer, though he was much older than his brother ever got the chance to become, he looked so much like Bastian that it caused me physical pain to look at him. It was like seeing the long-dead ghost of the man I once loved. I did my best to school my features to seem indifferent or even angry, anything but wounded.

"*You* are the one who turned him?" I managed to ask.

"I'm sorry, do you still not understand? Your precious Bastian didn't kill the majority of those people. I did. The difference being he couldn't control himself and I killed deliberately. I've always wondered how you decided *he* was the one responsible. If you were intimate for any length of time, surely you already knew what he was. So, what was it that finally made you kill him?"

I did my best to answer him matter-of-factly, but failed to keep the emotion from my voice. "I caught him devouring a child outside my cottage."

His smile was evil incarnate. "Ah. That'll do it. Strangely, he hid *you* from *me* the way he hid *me* from *you*. He only described a beautiful woman he was involved with *once*. I believe he was afraid of watching the two people he loved most tear each other apart. I was injured by a hunter a few days before you killed Bastian, otherwise I would have restrained him so close to the full moon. At least until he learned more control. The once famous Vallis d'Ulfric was quite the cunt, nearly killed me *twice*. But I'm getting off course here; I was telling you a story."

Maroc was right. This man was in love with the sound of his own voice. To say he was full of himself was an understatement. I guessed that when Vallis hunted him and accidentally left him alive the first time, he didn't realize he was the brother of The Beast. Otherwise, I'm sure he would have mentioned it to me.

"Vallis left me for dead and it took me a few years to fully recover. Once I was at full strength again I had a surprisingly difficult time finding you. It was almost as if you were protected by magic." He winked and I wanted to ram my boot up his arse.

"But I *did* get lucky enough to find your daughter and son-in-law."

I felt as if the wind had been knocked out of me. There was no hiding my pain, but I refused to speak.

"Oh, you didn't know that either? She was delicious, by the way. He was a bit tough for my tastes."

He continued to talk, but I lost track of what he was saying, lost in my grief and memories. Bella was with me that summer, learning more about hunting and how to fight. We performed a ritual together, to ask for the blessings of our ancestors. It was a rite of passage for the women in our family. My daughter had shared with me before we left that she was pregnant. She was excited and wanted a big family. They were going to add onto their cottage while we were gone and surprise Bella with the news when we came back.

We returned instead two months later to find the cottage nearly destroyed and our family in pieces. There was no addition to the cottage, and judging by their remains they were killed fairly soon after we left.

Part of me died that day. The woman I am now never recovered from picking up pieces of her daughter. I shielded Bella from seeing their remains, and I never told her about the pregnancy.

Confronted with this now … it was like having stitches ripped out before the wound could heal.

"After that, once I realized who they were and how close I finally was to my brother's killer, you disappeared."

I looked up when I realized he was still talking.

"No matter who I tortured or how many times I asked, no one seemed to know your name or where you lived. And yet, you were *famous*. I would hear people in taverns talking about you, *by name*, and then I couldn't remember it later. I tried having others listen on my behalf and they almost immediately forgot your name as well. It took me twelve years to find someone who was strong enough to even *begin* to crack through the veil of your spellwork."

"I was further delayed by that arsehole Vallis catching up with me for the second time. I heard he died of his injuries from our last encounter."

"I heard you had your head chopped off." I was surprised that I was able to speak again.

"And you didn't find that strange? That Bastian had a brother who also ended up as a werewolf? You *really* never put the pieces together?"

"I thought that somewhere along the way he must have attacked you. But you seem very satisfied with yourself about everything. Why don't you finish your story?" I said with a sneer of disgust. "Tell us how you survived."

"Vallis and his son were never great at decapitation."

At this Wolf gave a derisive snort.

"My head was still attached enough to eventually heal." When Gaston gestured to his throat I saw a red line that appeared to run all the way around his neck, as if the scar held his head onto his body. "He was never as thorough as you."

Images of what I'd done to insure Bastian was dead flashed through my mind, as I'm sure was his intent. The bastard.

"Why take the time to tell me all of this? Why waste your breath?"

He smiled and it took all of my strength to remain where I stood and not attack him. I wanted to knock every one of those dazzling white teeth down his throat, give him time to shit them out, and make him eat them again.

"Besides my obvious pleasure in seeing your misery? Because after thirty four years, I want you to know that you didn't finish the job you are so famous for. The Beast was not one man, but two. And if I'm being honest, I was always the stronger half. I will feast on your heart and then I will track down your granddaughter and eat her, cunt first."

Chapter Thirty Two

Islene

"You're forgetting the part where you have to go through me first," Wolf growled.

"Gladly."

Horror rose within me as Gaston tore open his tunic, grabbed the flesh of his chest, and tore it apart as easily as a second layer of cloth.

I took several steps back as he clawed his way out of his human skin, revealing the beast beneath. Flesh and clothing was cast aside while Gaston grew nearly as tall as Wolf.

They were nearly equal in height and muscle, making the other werewolves I'd seen, as well as the others present, seem small in comparison.

Gaston's transformation was barely complete when he leapt at Wolf. His claws and fangs seemed to grow longer in mid-air. When his massive jaws snapped closed over Wolf's forearm I winced at the sound of tearing flesh.

Though he roared in pain, Wolf dug his claws deep into Gaston's neck. When he pulled back Gaston's eyes glowed a deep red. *This* was The Beast as he had been described to me, many times, not my poor Bastian. Here was the devourer of livestock and humanity alike. *This* was the creature I should have killed along with his unfortunately cursed brother. For as much as it pains me to admit, even after all Gaston told me, I would *still* have killed Bastian. Even if he could not control himself, there is no going back from killing a child. The only thing I would have done differently, had I known that Gaston was the bigger monster, is hunt him down before he could find my daughter. But … I didn't know.

"You scratch like a bitch," Gaston said to him with a snarl, running a hand over the back of his neck.

"I'm looking for the scar. I could have sworn I saw it when you were running your mouth to the huntress," Wolf said.

Gaston's eyes widened as he barely dodged a slash of claws. *"You,"* he growled. "I knew your scent was familiar." He grinned lasciviously and licked his fingertips as he looked Wolf up and down. "Are you the result of *my* bite?"

Wolf only gave a low growl in response.

"Well, that's interesting. I don't remember biting you, but things happen in the heat of battle. Especially when you start to lash out at anything that moves."

Wolf lunged forward and tore a gash across one of Gaston's massive thighs. To my dismay I could already see the wound beginning to close. It would take a great deal of injuries in very quick succession to put this monster down at last.

"Tell me, are you the father or the son?"

"I'm going to find that scar," Wolf said, "and use it to pull you apart like a poorly stitched seam. *I'm* the one who didn't finish you the first time, and you never saw it coming."

A look of fury passed over Gaston's bestial face. An instant later the two alphas were a rolling mass of muscle, claws, and snapping jaws. One look around and I saw everyone's attention was focused on them.

I backed farther away, not only to stay out of the way of the fight, but to give myself the advantage of having no one at my back. I easily slipped out of leather strap we'd used to look as though I was restrained. I slipped a hand into my boot and gripped the hilt of my favorite dagger.

When I looked up I saw Bella, silent as death, perched atop one of the ruined walls. No one else appeared to have noticed her, for she was invisible to them until her first attack. Her eyes glowed red from the vampire blood and she had a small bottle of potion in one hand, ready to strike.

The alphas rolled to a stop and Gaston leapt to his feet first. Deep claw marks marred his chest and blood ran freely down his body.

"Have you truly come to fight daddy?" he mocked, pacing around the fire. "Only someone turned by me could be so strong. Why not join me ... *Maroc*?"

A few of the other werewolves gasped as Gaston confirmed what I was already convinced of. They may not have known who he was when he was referred to as Vallis' son, or perhaps they were not paying attention. But they were all certainly familiar with the name Maroc d'Ulfric.

"And now you've sealed the fate of your pack as well," Maroc said.

Chapter Thirty Three

Maroc

Hell was unleashed around me as silver daggers flew past my ears.

The other werewolves began to attack Islene and an instant later glass shattered and three werewolves burst into flames.

"Burn!" Bella yelled.

She jumped from the partial wall and rolled to her feet in the midst of the fray, descending upon them like a goddess of death. She quickly finished the three burning werewolves while they were distracted by the fire. I stopped to stare, not realizing what I'd done until I caught Gaston watching her as well. If this is how vampires fought, I never wanted to encounter one.

Howls echoed from farther out in the woods as more wolves came running at us from the darkness. Some were still mid-transformation. Others were already turned, having been ready from the start.

Gaston was momentarily distracted as flames erupted near him. I should have taken this opportunity to injure him as badly as possible, but I saw a woman who *had* to be his witch. She had a knife in her hand and she was running toward Bella's unguarded back.

The witch was well out of my reach, so I did the only thing I could. I grabbed a rock and threw it as hard as I could.

The rock struck her forehead with a resounding *crack*. The witch screamed and hit the ground. If I'd thought Gaston was angry before, I was mistaken.

I grew my claws longer and braced for his next attack as a flaming werewolf ran directly between us howling and screaming in agony.

Gaston lashed out and kicked him. When I held up my hands in an effort to dodge the fire I impaled the burning werewolf on my claws.

Gaston swept my legs from beneath me and I had only a moment to throw the werewolf aside or have his burning body fall on top of me. I rolled just in time to miss the stomp of Gaston's big clawed foot.

"I expected more of a fight," he said.

His next kick caught me in the ribs and sent me flying over the fire and into what remained of a stone wall.

Chapter Thirty Four

Bella

I was strangling a werewolf with my silver tipped whip when I saw Wolf go flying over the bonfire.

I was so focused on the werewolves who thought they were hidden beyond view that I did not hear what caused the fighting to spread. Even with my senses enhanced as they were, I could not focus on everything at once.

When my grandmother's daggers went flying, I took that as my signal to throw the potion. Just as she'd said, there was no simple way to extinguish witch's fire. *That* is a potion I must learn.

I held the whip with one hand, tightening my rip while I struggled to reach one of the blades at my waist. Searing pain spread down to my hand as the werewolf's teeth dug into my forearm.

Even after what my grandmother said about not being able to become infected, this scared me to the point of almost losing my grip on the whip. Years of training don't simply vanish after drinking some vampire blood.

The monster on top of me fought hard and I was amazed that I could hold on. When I finally got a grip on my blade I stabbed him in the throat several times, faster than I ever could have moved before.

Hot blood sprayed across my face and before I could stop myself I began to gulp it down. The werewolf's blood was the most divine thing I'd ever tasted. I tore into his throat with my knife and my teeth. Temporary or not, I definitely had a thirst for blood.

I shoved the wolf off of me and quickly got to my feet. I wiped my mouth on the back of my hand as I looked around for my next drink. When I noticed my torn sleeve I saw that the bite beneath was already healing.

I saw Wolf get to his feet and go charging back toward Gaston. I turned to watch their fight and was stabbed in the ribs. The dark haired witch was smiling, but only until she looked into my eyes.

I hit her with the back of my hand and laughed when she bounced off the crumbling wall. I stalked closer, feeling the hot blood soaking my clothes. She was bleeding from the forehead and had a big lump between her eyes.

"What are you?" she gasped.

"I assume the way I feel is because of the vampire blood; I have never delighted in anyone's suffering before. However—" I removed her blade from my ribs. "I've never had the opportunity to hurt someone who tried to kill my friend before."

I crouched beside her and smiled. "But you want to know what I am, witch? I am Perrin's friend." With those words I began to rip her apart in ways I never knew was possible with only my hands.

I was completely lost to the bloodlust until a werewolf head rolled past where I crouched, shredding the witch's flesh to ribbons.

"Bella!"

I looked up to see my grandmother, covered in blood as she retrieved her knives from a dead werewolf.

"You must pull yourself back," she said.

I released what remained of the witch and rose slowly.

"Fight it," she said. "Believe me when I tell you that I understand what you're feeling."

I gasped for air as I visibly shook with the need to rend flesh. "Did becoming what you are make werewolf blood taste better than candy?"

Her eyes widened. "No." She moved closer as she surveyed the bodies around me. "But I do sometimes get lost in my cravings for violence. The tearing of flesh with my teeth. The feel of bones breaking in my hands, just for the satisfaction of the *crunch* they make."

She smiled slightly and I suddenly understood what she had been fighting all these years.

I took a deep breath and backed away from the dead woman at my feet.

"What did I do to her?"

"Nothing less than what she deserved. She'd been sacrificing people in rituals and standing by while Gaston tortured them." She spat on the corpse and made a rude gesture. "*Fuck* her."

The sounds of screaming and flesh tearing brought our attention back to the ongoing battle of the alphas.

"Is *this* more what you expected?" Wolf roared.

Gaston was face down, crawling across the ground when Wolf fell on him, driving an elbow into his spine.

Gaston howled. Wolf gripped the back of his head in one massive hand and began to slam Gaston's face into the ground. "Is this the fight you wanted?"

The third time Gaston's face met the ground I heard a sickening crunch. When Wolf released him and slowly stood up, I didn't understand what he was doing. Gaston was still breathing!

Wolf looked to my grandmother. "Islene," he said softly, "for all he has done to you … all that you have lost. Would you like to kill The Beast?"

She paused, staring at the broken, bleeding monster and then slowly shook her head. "I killed my Beast long ago. Do what you promised him you would. Tear his head off."

His glowing amber eyes met mine. "Bella, he ate your parents …"

The question was unspoken but still I echoed her response.

"Tear his fucking head off."

He knelt beside Gaston and ran his long clawed fingertips over the back of the fallen werewolf's neck. Wolf combed through Gaston's thick fur as if looking for something. Finding what he sought, Wolf stabbed the claws of both hands into Gaston's neck.

There was a sound like cloth being torn. Gaston's eyes were suddenly open wide and he began to scream and fight, trying to throw Wolf from his back. But he was already weakened by numerous injuries and his struggles were futile.

With each rip of his flesh his screams echoed around us, until at last his enormous head was torn from his body.

I fell to my knees and vomited onto the already bloody grass.

"Ah, the vampire blood must be wearing off," my grandmother said.

I saw a finger amongst the torrent of blood I coughed up and heaved even harder.

"I had no idea the blood would affect you so strongly," she said. "For that much I *am* sorry. But you are still alive and whole."

"Never again," I gasped between retching. "*Fuck* vampire blood. I think I *ate* part of the witch."

While I continued to vomit blood from time to time, we surveyed the carnage.

"I count ten werewolves," Wolf said, tossing Gaston's head onto the fire.

"That's all that Perrin was aware of," my grandmother said.

"And the witch," I added. "Are we going to take any heads back as proof this nightmare has ended?"

"Well, not his," he said, gesturing to Gaston's head in the fire. "I'm not taking that chance again."

"I don't feel like dragging them back and we were already paid for the last hunt," my grandmother said.

Wolf looked around again. "We can't leave this massacre for someone to find, and this fire won't be enough to consume the remains."

I pulled two remaining bottles of witch's fire from my bag. "This should get the job done."

*****

Dawn broke over the land, casting a rose colored light over us as we watched the bodies burn.

"The Beast is truly gone," my grandmother said softly. "At last."

The early morning sun hit me fully and I might have collapsed if not for Wolf's big body to brace me from behind.

"That's the remaining effects of the vampire blood," she said. "Your strength will return by this evening and you should feel like yourself again by tomorrow."

I turned to Wolf and buried my face in the fur of his abdomen, because that is as high as I could reach.

"I'm a mess," he said.

It was true; he was covered in blood and injuries that were still healing.

"So am I."

When he wrapped me in his strong furry arms it was as if the world around us no longer existed.

"We survived," I said, holding him tightly.

"Only one alpha remains. Will you let him live?"

I looked up and saw he was talking to my grandmother. She smiled. "For as long as he makes my granddaughter happy."

Chapter Thirty Five

Belladonna

Maroc and I took our vows a week later in the castle courtyard, beneath the full wolf moon. The night was cool, the decorations were lavish and there was not a mushroom in sight.

The crowd danced and cheered as soft music drifted through the air and wine flowed freely. People were still talking about our wedding celebration. Apparently everyone had a wonderful time and no one except for the people directly involved ever knew werewolves were nearby that night.

The threat was ended and we could all finally relax.

"I have never seen anything more exquisite than your body in that dress," Maroc purred in my ear as his hand wrapped around my waist from behind.

The gown was a magnificent creation of red silk and lace. "It's the most beautiful thing I've ever worn," I said, putting my hand over his.

The entire moment felt too good to be real. Surely I would wake up soon.

"I can't wait to take it off of you," he said with a trace of growl in his deep voice.

Just then Cherry caught my attention and gestured for me to follow her. I excused myself and followed my friend inside the castle. We hadn't had a chance to speak alone since before the hunt, and after I was wrapped up in wedding preparations.

"You look anxious," I said. "Is everything all right? Is this about Perrin?"

She waved off my question and looked over her shoulder nervously. "Perrin and I are fine. He is chasing after a barmaid and I am with Armand, but that's not why I need to talk to you. You may already know this … in fact, I'm not sure after what I saw." She hesitated. "The Comte is — "

"Planning a surprise for you," he said, putting a big hand on my shoulder. "*That* is a gift I wish to give Bella alone. I assure you, she will enjoy it." He winked at Cherry and her face turned red as a beet.

"Very well." She gave a brief curtsy and quickly walked away.

"What was that about?" I asked.

"I believe Cherry may have seen a part of me I did not intend to share. But I also believe she is trustworthy."

"So long as it wasn't your cock," I teased.

"It definitely was *not*."

He swept me into his arms and I laughed with pure delight.

"I cannot wait to have my hands on you. The celebration will go on without us."

He carried me up the stairs at an inhuman pace, holding the long train of my dress in his hand to keep from tripping. The press of his lips against mine was a gentle promise as he closed the door with his foot.

He pulled back from me as his eyes bled to amber. I reached up to touch his face and he turned to press a kiss into my palm.

"I must tell Cherry that I already knew. I had you figured out sooner than you realize."

"Of course you did," he smiled as he trailed kisses up my arm.

"Of course I did," I repeated.

With a hand on each shoulder he turned me around and began to unlace my dress. He kissed each small expanse of flesh as it was revealed and in no time at all my clothes lay in a puddle of silk and lace at our feet.

I laughed softly and put one arm over my breasts. "You can't see all of me until I see all of you, remember?" I teased.

He walked around me slowly, letting his coat fall to the floor. I looked up into his amber eyes and he licked his lips as he began to unbutton his shirt with agonizing slowness. Next, he pulled the black ribbon from his hair and shook out his raven locks.

"Do you approve?" his deep voice rumbled.

"You are ..." I searched for the words to describe how beautiful he was and how much I wanted him. When words failed me I simply moved my arm, showing him my breasts.

His smile was scandalous.

"Yours," he said softly, finishing my sentence.

His hand trailed delicately over my shoulder as he walked around me again. He ran his fingers between my legs from behind and with one hand over my throat, slowly thrust them into my wet sex.

"Tell me what you want," he said before running his tongue along the side of my throat.

"My Wolf, my Stranger," I gasped. "I want you to fuck me until I scream."

"Mmmmm," he growled. "That won't take long."

He lifted me quickly, spreading my legs as he held me from behind. Having a man with the strength of a werewolf was something I could definitely get used to. Before I knew what was happening I had my face pressed against the door. He took my hands and pressed them flat on the door as I sat back against his big body like a chair.

With one hand he freed his cock while he cupped my breasts with the other. His growl of pleasure hummed along my skin as he nipped gently at the back of my neck before following the slight pinch with another kiss.

He thrust into me deep and hard and within moments I was screaming incoherently as he pounded me into the door.

For hours we moved from one piece of furniture to the next until we at last found ourselves in his enormous bed.

*****

I awoke late in the night to the sound of a fire crackling in the large hearth. I remembered I'd been dreaming about eating that evil witch and suddenly felt sick.

I rose slowly and slipped into Maroc's robe which was so large it trailed behind me.

I walked closer to the hearth to find him in full werewolf form reading by the fire. He was turning the page delicately with his claws and gently holding a small teacup in his other hand. The book, that was dwarfed by his big body, was resting on a pillow in his lap.

I'd forgotten it was the full moon and he *must* fully transform at some point. When he looked up at me I couldn't help but laugh. The sight before me was so ridiculous.

He looked down at himself and shrugged. "It *is* the full moon," he said.

He put his book and teacup on the table beside the chair.

"Is this the moment you've chosen to fully reveal yourself to me?" I said, laughing. "The time when you think I would *most* enjoy the revelation?"

He gestured to his body. "Are you saying you *aren't* enjoying this?"

I smiled and moved closer.

"I didn't mean to wake you," he said softly.

"You didn't. I think I was having a nightmare about eating part of that witch."

"I'm sorry," he said, reaching for me.

"It's all right." I curled up in his arms. "The dreams will pass. It's not as if I haven't seen my share of violence before."

I rested my face against his chest with a sigh. When he reached for the book again I asked, "Is that the one about sex with werewolves?"

I loved the sound of his deep laughter.

"No. Would you like me to find it?"

"I can't think of a better way to spend the night of the full moon, *Wolf*."

"Neither can I, little red."

THE END.

About the author:

This multi-published New York Times and USA Today bestselling author has been writing stories for her own entertainment since she was a child. Tracey has always been drawn to the macabre, with a fondness for anything with fangs. She writes what she enjoys reading in the hopes that others will enjoy her stories as well. Her main goal as a writer is to put emotions into words. She wants people to feel something when they read her work.

T.K. Hardin is the name she uses for her erotic horror stories.

http://www.traceyhkitts.com/

https://www.facebook.com/grablifebythefangs

Claim your free copy of Wicked City at www.traceyhkitts.com/free-book-offer/

Other books by Tracey H. Kitts

The Lilith Mercury, Werewolf Hunter Series
Red
Object of My Affection
The Dread Moon
Original Sin
A Dream Forbidden
The Bleeding Heart
After Dark

Bound by Blood series
Bound by Blood: Oriana's Curse
Bound by Blood: Demon's Embrace
Bound by Blood: Dragon Slayer Dreams
Bound by Blood: Enter the She-Dragon

Notte Oscura series
Frank and The Werewolf Tamer
Night Touch
Psychopomp & Circumstance

There's No Place series
There's No Place: Homecoming
There's No Place: Embracing the Beast
There's No Place: Interfering with Destiny
There's No Place: Claiming the Wolfman

Tris Grima series
Love me HARD
Bite of Frost

Book Three TBA

Unseelie of Atlanta series
Shaman's Touch
Wounded Heart
<u>*Rhiannon Frost Trilogy: (TBA)*</u>
Lord of Frost
Frosty Reception
Lady of Frost

Books unrelated to series
Necromancer
Bitten
Eden
Diary of an Incubus
Wicked City
Sex Symbol
Till the break of Dawn
Three Days of Night
Fate's Embrace
Raven's Destiny
Touch of an Incubus
The Eternal Kiss
Howl for me
Beautiful Nightmare
Once Upon a Full Moon
Sacrifice
Dragon Charmer
Bloodlines
Wolf Cove

Writing as T.K. Hardin

Dracula: In The Flesh
Frankenstein: Unleashed
Of Shadow and Blood

Manufactured by Amazon.ca
Bolton, ON

45658628R00162